PICTURE PERFECT

White Dove Romances

9612

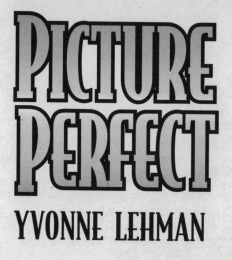

PICTURE PERFECT

YVONNE LEHMAN

BETHANY HOUSE PUBLISHERS
MINNEAPOLIS, MINNESOTA 55438

Published by Bethany House Publishers
A Ministry of Bethany Fellowship, Inc.
11300 Hampshire Avenue South
Minneapolis, Minnesota 55438

Printed in the United States of America.

Library of Congress Cataloging-in-Publication Data

Lehman, Yvonne.
    Picture perfect / Yvonne Lehman.
        p.   cm. — (White dove romances ; 4)
    Summary: When Scott's cousin Cissy wins a modeling contest, sixteen-year-old Natalie is invited to join them on a trip to New York City, where she has a chance to examine her feelings for Scott and witness the power of Cissy's faith.
    ISBN 1–55661–708–9
    [1. Christian life—Fiction. 2. Interpersonal relations—Fiction. 3. Models (Persons)—Fiction.
4. New York (N.Y.)—Fiction.] I. Title. II. Series: Lehman, Yvonne. White dove romances ; 4.
PZ7.L5322Pi   1996
[Fic]—dc21   96–45909
                                              CIP
                                              AC

My deepest gratitude to
Lori—for her invaluable insight
Howard—for his helpful advice
Cindy and David—for their modeling inspiration
Anne—for her expert editing
and
the Mariott Marquis—for the fabulous background.

YVONNE LEHMAN is the award-winning author of thirteen published novels, including seven inspirational romances, two contemporary novels, a biblical novel, *In Shady Groves*, and three young adult novels. She and her husband, Howard, have four grown children and five grandchildren, and they make their home in the mountains of North Carolina.

One

Natalie Ainsworth had been waiting all evening for just the right moment to spring the news.

Now was definitely *not* the right moment!

"Can you believe that score? Three to ze-rooow—zilch—zip!" screeched Stick Gordon, flopping into a booth at the Pizza Palace.

"Well, scoot over, dork!" demanded Ruthie Ryan, her riot of red curls springing around her face. "The rest of us want to sit, too. That *is* what you're doing, I take it?"

Stick was sprawled out on the seat, his long, lanky legs taking up half the space under the table. As Shawnee High's ace basketball player, he might be able to get away with his usual goofy stuff during the spring, but this was *football* season!

"You heard her, buddy." Sean Jacson hoisted Stick up by his three-inch brush of hair and wrestled him into the corner, where Stick went into his hyena impression, baying at the harvest moon shining through the window. Ruthie rolled her big brown eyes but slid in beside Stick, followed by Sean. They were quickly joined on the other side by Marcie Fields, Craig Harman, and Philip Sloan,

7

three of the other kids who had stopped by everyone's favorite watering hole after the homecoming game.

"We can't all cram into that one booth," Natalie observed, pulling out a chair at a table nearby. "If you recall, this was a group decision." The others—Twila Jones and Colby Reid—grabbed two more chairs and settled in beside her.

"I need food!" Stick beat on the table with his fist, then grinned broadly when a waitress, wearing a Pizza Palace apron, hurried over to take their order.

"Yeah, our pal here is a bottomless pit," Sean put in, "so you'd better give us a rundown of everything on the menu."

"I don't know these people," Natalie groaned, then smiled at the girl she recognized as having graduated last spring. "Don't pay any attention to them, Phyllis."

Phyllis Haney returned her smile, then glanced down at the order pad in her hand. Was she working her way through college? Natalie wondered. Or was she planning to be a waitress for the rest of her life?

But it wasn't really Phyllis's future Natalie was worried about—it was her own. She ignored the nagging uncertainty and placed her order, then listened to the excited babble of her friends as they replayed every move of the football game.

"Did you see that awesome pass Chuck Henry made?"

"Yeah, and who would have ever thought old Lead-Legs Baird would have come through with that touchdown!"

Natalie was just as excited as they were—but not about the game! She waited until two steaming giant-sized pizzas—extra-extra cheese, thin crust—were served and the rest of the gang was chomping away before she launched her announcement. "You'll never guess where I'm going to spend the Thanksgiving holiday."

"Thanksgiving?" Ruthie cut her eyes over at her best friend. "Shawnee High has just beaten our biggest rival in the game of the year by a field goal and you want to talk about *Thanksgiving*?"

"Girl, this is only the middle of October!" Twila reminded her.

"She *said* we'd never guess." Stick crammed a piece of pizza into his mouth. "Just ignore her." At the scowls, he lifted his hand, chewed quickly, and swallowed.

Natalie smiled mysteriously, refusing to be daunted by these delay tactics. She could wait.

Ruthie was the first to cave in. "Okay, okay, we give up. Besides, you'll never let us rest until you tell us."

Pausing, with all eyes now on her, Natalie plunged in. "I'm going with Scott to . . . ta da—" she spread her hands—"New York City!"

"Natalie Ainsworth!" blurted Ruthie, who knew her better than anyone in the whole world. "We all know your parents won't let you go off to New York City with Scott Lambert. They want you to be 'sweet sixteen' and under their watchful eyes forever."

"Too late. I've been seventeen for several months now. Besides, Scott and I won't be there alone. Cissy's going, too. So are her mom and Scott's mom—they're sisters, you know. You remember, I went to their lake house this summer . . . when Katlyn was hurt."

At the mention of Katlyn Chander, there was an awkward silence.

"Speaking of rivals," Twila began, her dark eyes skeptical in her smooth brown face, "how could you stand watching Katlyn with Scott at halftime tonight?"

Twila's boyfriend, Colby, nudged her and frowned, and Twila covered her mouth with her hand. "Oops!"

Natalie felt a twinge. In the entire history of Shawnee High, Katlyn Chander had been the first girl in a wheelchair—probably the *only* girl in a wheelchair—to be elected homecoming queen. After the accident, everyone had rallied around her, and now—even with a few scars—she was more popular than ever.

"Oh, that wasn't a real date." Natalie shrugged, hoping she sounded more convincing than she felt. "Katlyn has vowed she's not going to date *anybody* until she's up on crutches, so she asked Scott to be her escort just so everyone would know she's not still holding a grudge against the Lamberts."

"Then why didn't she ask Zac?" Stick wanted to know. "After all, *he's* the one to blame for putting her in that wheelchair in the first place!"

The whole awful scene came rushing back. Scott's older brother, Zac, drunk at the wheel of his bright red sports car. Katlyn, speared in the headlights, then pinned against the front of the grocery store in Lake Oakwood.

"Frankly, I don't know *why* she didn't ask him. I know he's been working with her in Rehab since the accident. Maybe it's because Zac's still on everybody's black list. Anyway, tonight was supposed to be Homecoming, not a rehash of last summer's scandal." Feeling a little defensive, she added, "If you must know, Scott checked it out with me first, and I told him I didn't mind. Besides, we're not going steady, or anything like that." *Not that I wouldn't love to be going steady with the best-looking guy at Shawnee High,* she admitted to herself, taking a long sip of her cola.

Apparently satisfied with her answers, they all dug into their pizza again. Natalie was pretty sure she understood Scott's motives for escorting Katlyn to the game. It was the decent thing to do. He and Natalie had been in the car when his brother had lost control of the car and run up on the curb. So he'd been around to check on Katlyn from the beginning—even when she wasn't speaking to Zac. It made sense.

Still. . . . She gulped her soda, feeling it fizz in her stomach. What if Scott was beginning to like Katlyn more than he would admit . . . even to himself?

Natalie glanced across at Ruthie. She could read her friend like an encyclopedia. From the look on the redhead's face, she knew Ruthie didn't trust Katlyn any further than she could see her!

But Katlyn has grown up a lot since the accident, Natalie thought, trying to be fair. *She even admits she needs God in her life. But I suppose that doesn't change the fact that she'd really like to snag Scott as a boyfriend.*

"Well, anyway, *I'm* the one Scott invited to New York," Natalie finished aloud.

With the excitement of the game dying down, the conversation turned to Natalie's trip. "What's the occasion, Nat?" Twila wanted to know.

"It's really Cissy's trip. She and Scott are cousins, you know, and—"

"Yeah, we know." Ruthie sighed.

Who *didn't* know Cissy Stiles? Last year's homecoming queen, with her corn-silk hair and her big baby blues. Daughter of one of the wealthiest families in town. Leader of the "in" crowd at school before she graduated in the spring. Not only that, but she had plenty of brains, too—except the time she'd tried to elope with Ron Miler and had been trapped in the tornado that touched down in Garden City. And now, thanks to the White Dove pin Natalie had given her, Cissy claimed, she'd turned her life over to the Lord.

"Well," Natalie began, "several months ago—before the storm and Katlyn's accident—Cissy entered her photograph in a national model search. But with everything that happened, she forgot all about it. . . ."

"Get to the point, girl," Twila urged.

"The point is—she's one of the top-ten finalists!" The entire gang gaped—pizza and all. "She gets all expenses paid to New York for the Dream Teen Model Search competition, tickets to a Broadway show, and a $500 shopping spree at Macy's."

"Wow! What does she get if she *wins*?" Stick asked.

"There'll be three winners," Natalie went on. "They get a contract with the modeling agency sponsoring the search. Cissy says that just about cinches the fact that the winners will be instant celebs, since it's one of the largest agencies in the world."

"Boy, some people have all the luck," complained Marcie, putting her elbows on the table and dropping her head into her hands.

"It's not just luck," Natalie said. "Cissy works on her looks." She glanced at the remains of their late-night feast. "For one thing, she never pigs out on pizza. . . ." There were a few groans from the girls. "And she takes acting classes," she added, thinking of the summer theater production, when Cissy had stolen the show. "Oh, I forgot to mention that the winners also receive a $10,000 scholarship to the college of their choice."

Sean, who had been quiet until now, slammed his hands against the Formica tabletop. "And *I'm* having to work to make it through my senior year of high school!"

Ruthie, sitting beside him, squeezed his arm. Everyone knew about Sean's parents splitting up.

Natalie sympathized, but it was really hard to put herself in his place. Practically *no*body these days had the kind of family life she had. A mom and dad who still acted like a couple of lovestruck teenagers. Three younger sisters who always got along great—well, *almost* always. "Anyway, Scott wants to check out photography schools in New York. Their moms are going along, so—" she couldn't hold back her broad smile— "I'm invited."

"When do you leave?" Marcie asked.

"Right before Thanksgiving."

Twila's brown cheeks dimpled. "Cool!"

"Hey, why is New York called the Big Apple?" Stick demanded, drawing attention to himself again.

But before Natalie could tell him she didn't know, the door burst open. Loud cheers went up as the football team rushed in, and the patrons of the Pizza Palace began to whistle and applaud. Several of the cheerleaders, whose boyfriends played on the team, were with them.

"Where's Amy, Nat?" Stick's expression was pained as he gawked at the incoming crowd. "She's the prettiest cheerleader on the whole squad!" It was nothing new for Stick to ask about Natalie's beautiful younger sister. The poor guy had had it bad ever since the day he'd first noticed her.

"Oh, she left early for a slumber party with some girlfriends."

"Guess she's still too young for me," he moaned pathetically.

"Afraid so," Natalie replied, spreading her hands helplessly. "She's not even fifteen yet—and we're not allowed to date until we're sixteen. Sorry, Stick."

"Bummer! I don't get it. Your parents won't let her go out with me—one of the church guys—but they'll let you go off to New York with Scott Lambert, who doesn't even go to our church."

"But he's in the youth group," Natalie reminded him. "And we'll be well protected. Scott's mom and aunt promised my folks they'd watch us every minute—with binoculars, no doubt!" She waited for the whoop of laughter to subside. "Anyway, Scott and I know about crime in the big city. We're not about to take any chances."

"That means you're aware of the worms that can get into apples—the fatter the apple, the bigger the worm." Stick chuckled at his own joke.

Natalie laughed, too, not daring to ask what he meant by that. She remembered something her twelve-year-old sister, Sarah, had said about Stick Gordon: "He may be the class clown . . . but sometimes he makes a lot of sense."

It had crossed Natalie's mind, more than once, that—finally—she and Scott would have some time alone—to find out what they meant to each other. She deliberately squelched a prick of conscience. Feeling her cheeks flush, she was grateful when Phyllis came up with the bill and asked, "You guys want anything else?"

It was on the way home, before dropping Ruthie off at Sean's request, that Natalie began to squirm.

"There was a lot of joking around tonight, Nat," her friend began, "but you do realize that pickpockets and muggers aren't the only villains in a great, big, beautiful city like New York, don't you? What about temptation? It'll be pretty romantic up there. . . ."

Natalie moaned. "Not you, too!"

"Hey, remember me?" Ruthie's brown eyes glinted gold in the moonlight shining through the windshield. "I'm the one who confessed that sometimes, when Sean is holding me, I don't want him to let me go."

"Ruthie! Don't you *dare* spoil this for me!"

"Well, we've always been honest with each other, haven't we? Who warned me about going steady with Sean? All those temptations, you said. Well, you were right. But I have to face my mom and dad when I come in from a date. And then there's always Monster standing by to give me the third degree: 'Did he kiss you? Did he kiss you?' Honestly, sometimes my little brother drives me crazy!" Ruthie rolled her eyes. "And don't forget the youth group . . . and our white doves." She smiled as Natalie's glance caught hers. "And as if all that weren't enough—I've got *you*! But who are *you* going to answer to in that fabulous place?"

"You mean besides my conscience and God?" Natalie stepped on the brake and came to a screeching stop in front of Ruthie's house.

"Oh, don't be smug with me. I'm just trying to save your reputation, that's all. You're going to New York with the most gorgeous guy at Shawnee High . . . and you're not worried about temptation?"

"Hey, wait a minute!" Natalie switched off the engine and draped her arm over the steering wheel. "You're saying *Scott* is the most gorgeous—"

Ruthie waved away Natalie's words. "Oh, pooh! Sean is my guy, and I'd be out with him right now if he hadn't had to work evenings at the warehouse." She stuck out her lower lip in a pout. "But we're talking about you and Scott here. And I happen to know you're in love with him . . . so you'd better watch your step."

Natalie sighed and shifted her position under the wheel. "I'm not so sure he feels the same way. Besides"—she lifted the collar of her blue turtleneck and held out the pin—a tiny white dove, wings spread— "we've both taken the pledge to remain sexually pure until marriage."

"Yeah. So the devil will *really* be after you!"

"You seem to know a lot about it."

Ruthie grinned. "A little. Especially since Sean's parents' divorce. He's having a really tough time, Nat. He needs me so much. It's a good thing we've been studying about how to say no in youth group. It's also great having a friend like you to be accountable to." She paused, then leaned over to look Natalie right in the eye. "Now, don't tell me you've never been tempted. . . ."

"To be honest, Ruthie, we haven't had much of a chance to be. We were in the house together during the tornado, but we were hardly alone—not with three sisters and Rose's dog, Pongo, to keep us company! And at the lake, he was worried about his mom's drinking problem . . . then Katlyn's accident. . . ."

"But in the Big Apple, it's gonna be sheer enchantment."

Natalie sighed. "Just thinking about it is sheer enchantment." She could feel little goosebumps rising on her arms.

Ruthie squinted through half-closed lids. "Hmmm . . . maybe you should leave your White Dove pin unclasped so it'll stick him if he gets too close."

"Ruthie Ryan, don't you think I have any morals at all?"

"Yep. As many as I do. But . . . like I said, there are weak moments. When you're wrapped in the arms of the one you love . . ." she hugged herself, her head back against the seat, "you tend to forget. . . ."

"Okay, okay. You've made your point. Now, out! I've got to get up early in the morning and do my chores, then I'm going shopping."

"Shopping?" Ruthie perked up.

Even in the moonlight, Natalie could see her friend's eyes dancing. If there was anything Ruthie Ryan liked to do . . . "I'm really sorry . . . but I promised Cissy." Uh-oh. From the look on Ruthie's face, Natalie had struck sparks.

"Well! Who'd ever have thought you'd be going to the mall with Cissy Stiles?"

"Not me," Natalie admitted. "But, Ruthie, you'll always be my best friend, you know that."

There was a pause that seemed to stretch into next week before Ruthie said anything. "It's going to be sad—after graduation—people going their separate ways. . . ."

"That's six months away—longer, counting next summer."

"Yeah, but you're already going places."

"Ruthie?" Natalie put out her hand. "Friends forever?"

Ruthie nodded, grasped the outstretched hand for a moment, then was her cheery self again. "Night. Call me the minute you get home with your new rags."

Natalie laughed. *Rags?* They would be anything but rags. Cissy's taste was New York all the way.

Driving home with the light of the full moon making the crisp autumn night almost as bright as day, Natalie tried to push aside the disturbing thoughts that buzzed in her head like a hive of bees. Was she really in love with Scott Lambert? Or was he falling for Katlyn Chander? As for being wrapped in his arms, Natalie hadn't a clue as to how *that* would feel. Except for holding hands a time or two and a little peck on the cheek, he'd never even touched her. But the thought that bugged her most was what Stick had said at the Pizza Palace.

"Oh, please, Lord," she murmured as she drove toward home, "don't let there be a big, fat worm in the Big Apple!"

Two

Jim Ainsworth whistled when Natalie walked into the kitchen for breakfast. "What's cooking, good-looking?"

"Oh, Dad." She hated it when he said things like that. As far as she was concerned, she was about as ordinary looking as a girl could get. Light brown hair, still sun-streaked from the summer. Blue eyes. Average height. Average weight. Nothing special.

But her three sisters were staring at her as if she had just grown an extra head. "Oh, you mean this old thing." Looking down, she held out the skirt of a denim shirtwaist. Most Saturdays she threw on the first thing she came to in her closet—usually a pair of jeans and an old T-shirt. "I'm going shopping with Cissy Stiles, and I just thought a dress would make it easier to try on things."

"I think you're really pretty, Natalie," little sister Rose spoke up. "So why didn't you get voted on for the homecoming court, like Amy?"

Before Natalie could think how to respond, twelve-year-old Sarah, the no-nonsense sibling, replied for her, "Amy's a cheerleader. Cheerleaders get lots of

19

votes because everybody knows them. Besides, Amy can do a Chinese split."

Amy quirked her lip. "And you're saying *that's* the only reason I got elected?"

Sarah shrugged. "All I'm saying is that you're popular."

"Oh." Amy might not be convinced, but she let it go.

Natalie exchanged a quick grin with her dad. Sarah was a born diplomat. She could skirt a potentially dangerous comment as easily as she had learned to sidestep a block on the basketball court—thanks to Stick Gordon's tutoring.

"Oh, everybody knows you're beautiful, Amy." Rose speared a syrupy bite of pancake and popped it into her rosebud mouth.

At that moment, Jill Ainsworth walked into the room, carrying the morning paper. "*All* my girls are beautiful in their own way."

Mom had been up for hours doing her aerobics routine. She was still sweaty. But that didn't stop Dad, who grabbed her free hand and pulled her over for a morning kiss. "And where do you think they got all that beauty?" He narrowed his gaze and eyed her up and down. "Even in *that* getup!"

"Oh, you." She gave him a playful shove. "How's a girl to stay young and beautiful if she doesn't work at it?"

Her parents could be a little sickening sometimes, Natalie thought, although she was secretly glad they loved each other that much. Still, she sure hoped she didn't give herself away every time she looked at Scott the way her mother did when she looked at Dad.

"Look who made the paper today," Jill was saying as she unfolded the newspaper and dropped it on the table. She spread it out for everyone to see.

They crowded around to read the caption under the half-page spread in the sports section: "Shawnee High's Homecoming Court Shines in Half-Time Ceremonies." Amy, looking really great, smiled up at them.

Natalie recalled how her sister had left the squad early to change into her evening gown. She'd taken down her long ponytail and fluffed her hair around her shoulders. But she hadn't needed much time for primping. With her clear skin and thick dark lashes fringing her eyes, Amy hadn't had to do much more than add a little lip gloss.

But it wasn't Amy's picture that grabbed Natalie's attention. It was Katlyn's—with Scott standing behind her wheelchair. To accommodate her problem, the other girls, holding long-stemmed roses, had also been seated, their escorts behind them. Scott, in a black tux that made his wavy hair and eyes appear even darker, looked sensational.

Unfortunately, so did Katlyn! Natalie had never seen the girl so radiant, with her black hair wreathed around her face like a cloud. It had grown out nicely since the accident, when her scalp had been shaved in at least two places so the doctors could stitch up deep gashes. Her white dress, spangled with beads, caught the light and reflected a silvery shimmer.

During the convertible ride around the stadium, Natalie remembered, Katlyn had been perched on the top of the backseat, with Scott beside her to hold her steady. Her shoulders had been bare until he'd reached over to place a white fluffy coat around them. Natalie hadn't missed the fact that he'd held it there while Katlyn continued to smile and wave at the crowd, saving her biggest smiles for Scott.

"Hey, let me," Amy was saying, jerking Natalie's attention from her memory of that tender little scene. "You guys act like you've never seen me before."

"Oh, I saw you all right," Jim said as the others moved back and Amy crowded in. "It's just hard to believe my little girls are growing up so fast."

"Then does that mean I can date?" Amy asked expectantly.

"Not a chance. You've got more than a year to go yet, so be patient."

"I think I look a lot older than fourteen," she pressed.

"So does your mother, but *she* can't date, either."

Jill grabbed a dishtowel and playfully swatted her husband on the backside. Everyone giggled, except Amy, who was still reliving that magical night.

"Indian summer!" Natalie breathed in the crisp morning air shortly before nine o'clock as she stepped out onto the front porch. The sun, filtering through the branches of the big maple, turned the leaves to gold and flame-red as a few more broke loose and drifted to the ground. Above, cream-puff clouds floated lazily in the deep blue sky. God always outdid himself in Garden City in the fall, she thought.

And here came another one of His best creations—Cissy Stiles—driving up in her navy Audi with the baby-blue interior that matched her eyes.

For a split second, Natalie felt the same kind of intimidation she'd felt last year, when Cissy was a senior and she, a junior, at Shawnee High. But everything had changed since then. She shook off the old fears and hopped into the front seat.

Cissy already looked like a supermodel in her black jumper with white baby T, silver chain bracelet, black hose, and black dressy shoes.

"Thanks for offering to take me shopping, Cissy." Natalie fastened her seat belt. "I know we still have plenty of time, but I've never been anywhere so special before and—"

"No problem, kiddo. We've got to do this up right for our trip to the Big Apple."

"By the way"—Natalie glanced over at Cissy, who was adjusting her rearview mirror—"do you know how New York got its nickname?"

"Hmmm." Cissy shrugged and pulled away from the curb. "Never thought of it. I'll have to check it out."

Well, there was at least *one* thing Cissy Stiles didn't know! Natalie leaned back in the bucket seat and closed her eyes. Just talking about New York sent delicious shivers along her spine. "How's college going?" she asked at last, opening her eyes and sitting up.

"The drama club is great, and I've got a lead role in a play, but the rest is sort of ho-hum."

"I'm surprised you settled for a local college."

Cissy laughed. "So am I. I'd planned to go to acting

school in New York, you know, and make it big as a model or actress. But you know that story . . . how I was eloping with Ron when the tornado literally turned all my plans upside down. When I finally came to my senses—thanks to *you*"—she shrugged—"it was too late to apply anywhere but locally."

"And now, you're going to New York for a modeling contest! God sure works in mysterious ways, doesn't He?"

Cissy glanced over at Natalie. "I'll say. To think, I turned to Him as a last resort, when He's the One with all the answers in the first place! Isn't it wild? I'm going to New York, after all . . . and the one who helped save my life is going with me!"

Natalie squirmed a little in her seat. She hadn't done a thing for Cissy that anyone else wouldn't have done under the circumstances. She'd just happened to be around when Cissy really needed someone.

When Cissy turned in at the mall, a little doubt popped up to mar Natalie's perfect day. Even though her mom had let all the relatives know about the trip and had asked that they give Natalie money as an early Christmas present, Natalie was worried about how to spend it. Cissy, the only child of a very successful hospital administrator, lived in Garden Acres—the most exclusive area of town—and dressed like it. Even with more money than usual in her purse, Natalie was afraid she still couldn't measure up to Cissy's high standards.

As if reading her mind, Cissy led her to one of the less expensive shops in the mall and rummaged through the racks. "Look at this." She held up a white baby T much like her own. "The trick is to choose things you can wear for casual or dressy."

"Really?" Natalie was surprised.

"I do it all the time."

"Oh, Cissy, I don't think I've ever seen you wear the same thing twice."

"That's because my modeling classes have taught me how to mix and match."

"You could have fooled me. But that little tip will sure come in handy, since I don't exactly have a fortune to spend."

Cissy laughed. "Wouldn't matter if you did. There's no sense in buying expensive clothes if you can get the same thing for less."

For the next hour or so, they meandered through almost every shop in the mall. Natalie had never enjoyed shopping so much, learning to compare prices and coordinate pieces instead of buying the first thing she saw. She'd had no idea how many different looks she could create with a few basic pieces.

"Now all we need is one really groovy jacket to pull everything together," Cissy said, looking around.

"You're really great to help me like this."

Cissy's smile was genuine. "It's the least I can do after all you did for me. I'll never forget the night you gave me that little white dove to hang on to, reminding me that God's Spirit was with me in the storm." She chuckled. "And in more ways than one!"

Cissy couldn't feel any better about it than Natalie did. That night had been a turning point for many people in Garden City. And here were three of them now. . . .

At a nearby rack, looking through the sale items,

were Ruthie, Marcie, and Lana.

"Hi, guys," Natalie said, walking over to them.

"Hi." It was a halfhearted greeting, and Natalie wondered why—until she noticed they were looking her up and down. It probably wasn't just the fact that she was overdressed for a Saturday morning. It was that she'd chosen to hang out with Cissy. This time last year, she and Ruthie would have avoided Cissy Stiles like the plague, assuming the older girl preferred not to associate with "peasants."

"Find anything?" Natalie asked, trying to make conversation while Cissy picked through another rack.

Seeing the load of packages and shopping bags Natalie was holding, Ruthie quipped, "Not *that* much."

Natalie shifted nervously, wishing she could hide her stuff. Why was she embarrassed to run into her best friend? Ruthie understood, didn't she? "This is early Christmas. The trip . . . you know."

"Yeah, sure." Ruthie wouldn't look at her, but turned to her other friends, pulling a dress from the rack. "Hey, Lana, look at this. Didn't you say you needed something to wear to the youth group party?"

Lana fingered the velvety fabric, then glanced at the price tag. "Well, it may be on sale, but it's still beyond my budget."

"Oh, don't worry. We'll find something at one of the other stores. See ya," Ruthie called over her shoulder to Natalie as they left the shop.

Natalie felt her heart sink, and the sensation didn't go away, even when Cissy found a to-die-for leopard-print jacket and lifted it for Natalie's inspection with a triumphant grin.

Natalie was feeling a little better by the time she got home and spread her purchases on the living room sofa. As her mom and sisters gathered around, she explained how the pieces could be interchanged. There was a longish winter white skirt, a short velvet one, a long-sleeved angora sweater, an ivory satin blouse, one dress—a burgundy panné velvet, a black quilted drawstring jacket, black pants, and the leopard-print jacket. Most everything could be worn either casual or chic.

"I paid more for each piece than I'd planned to . . . but Cissy pointed out how many more outfits I'd have by mixing and matching."

"How much?" her mom wanted to know. Natalie wasn't surprised. In a family of six, that question was asked more than any other. She could just hear the calculator whirring in Jill Ainsworth's brain.

Natalie grinned. "Would you believe I got all this for less than my Christmas money?"

"I can believe you're not going to find much of anything under the tree," her dad chimed in.

"Oh, I can't think of a single thing I need now"—*unless it's Scott Lambert*—"except maybe a little spending money for souvenirs and a few little gifts for the family." At that, Rose's face lit up with anticipation.

The Stileses and the Lamberts would be paying all Natalie's expenses in New York, of course, including tickets to a Broadway play. But she figured that they were just trying to make up for the fiasco at Lake Oakwood, where she'd been a houseguest when Scott's brother had gotten drunk and nearly killed Katlyn Chander.

"Well, you'll have to *earn* your spending money, young lady," Jill cautioned, "beginning with supper. How about peeling the potatoes?"

"Thanks, Mom." Great idea her parents had had— paying their four daughters for doing extra chores around the house. "If it's okay with you, I'll just leave my new things here for a while. Maybe Ruthie will come over after supper."

But after supper, Ruthie had a convenient excuse to turn her down. "Sorry," she told Natalie coolly when she phoned, "Marcie and Lana just left, and I'm going out with Sean tonight, so I have to get ready. 'Bye." The message was short and not too sweet.

"Well, come over whenever you can." Natalie replaced the receiver slowly. *This trip to New York may be more expensive than I thought—if it costs me my best friend!*

For the next three weeks, Natalie barely saw Ruthie except in class. Natalie was either cramming for midterms, doing extra chores to earn spending money for the trip, or meeting with Andy and Stephanie Kelly, the youth group leaders. This year's holiday project— collecting food and toys for single parents and their children—was pretty ambitious. It was going to take a lot of coordination, and as the president of the youth group, Natalie had her work cut out for her.

Even with all the activity, though, time seemed to poke by.

The weekend before Natalie left for New York, Ruthie finally showed up. "Sorry I didn't come sooner.

But I knew you'd been busy"—she dropped her gaze to the new clothes laid out on a chair—"and I've been *available* to spend time with Sean—though he hasn't been around much. He's really down about his parents fighting all the time."

"Why aren't you guys out tonight?"

Ruthie sighed and flopped down on the bed beside the suitcase Natalie was packing. "He had to work an extra shift at the food-chain warehouse." She paused, as if wondering whether to go on. "He's working so much his grades have fallen, Nat. He just doesn't have time to study, and he expects *me* to help him," she wailed, burying her curly head in a pillow, then popped back up, looking so much like a forlorn puppy that Natalie almost laughed out loud. "I mean it, Nat. I'm trying . . . but I don't have your brains."

"Oh, Ruthie, stop putting yourself down. You're plenty smart."

"Well, I've bombed out so far. I just can't get through to him."

Natalie picked up the ivory blouse and folded it. "If the trained teachers can't, how can you expect to do any better?"

"*Sean* expects me to."

Natalie packed the blouse and straightened—as much as the low ceiling in her tiny attic room would allow. "Ruthie, the responsibility is Sean's, not yours."

Her friend looked offended. "I thought Christians were supposed to help each other."

"Sure we are, but we can't always *solve* another person's problems. There wasn't much I could do about Scott's mother's alcoholism this summer. Helen Lambert had to do that herself."

"But you stuck by Scott."

"True," Natalie admitted.

"Well . . ." Ruthie tugged at a pillow, pulled it under her chin, and sat up. "I'm sticking by Sean . . . even if some of his so-called friends treat him differently now that he's got problems."

"Good for you!" Seeing that her friend was still upset, Natalie tried to cheer her up. "Oh, have I told you that Cissy's going to be riding in the Macy's Thanksgiving Day Parade?"

Ruthie narrowed her eyes. "How did she manage that?"

"She called me this afternoon and told me that Macy's has offered to let the ten finalists ride on their float. It'll be good publicity for the store since the girls will probably be wearing clothes they'll buy with their $500 gift certificates."

The news didn't seem to do much for Ruthie's sour mood. "And you're going to get to be right there and stand on the sidewalk and wave to her."

Natalie sat down beside her on the bed. "Ruthie . . . are you jealous?"

"You'd better believe it!" Ruthie exploded in a flurry of red hair and flashing brown eyes. "*I* used to be your best friend. But, baby, you're sure moving up in the world!"

When Ruthie got like this, it was always better to let her cool down. So it was a minute before Natalie answered her. "Sure I am. My life's ambition has always been to stand on the sidewalks of New York City and wave to Cissy Stiles."

At the ridiculous idea, Ruthie giggled in spite of herself. Pretty soon the two were holding on to each other, cracking up in howls of laughter.

When their hysterics finally subsided and they were lying, side by side, on the bed, Ruthie sighed. "Still, things—and people—seem to be changing." Out of the corner of her eye, Natalie could see that little-girl pout again. "You'll forget all about me in the Big Apple."

"No way!" Natalie meant it. She'd never have a better girl friend than Ruthie Ryan. But that didn't include the possibility of *boy*friends.

She had to admit she'd never felt about a guy the way she felt about Scott Lambert. Sometimes, just hearing his name was like hearing the entire band doing their special number at half time. Other times, it was more like a whisper. Funny how love could be strong as that tornado that had roared through Garden City, yet soft as a baby's breath. How powerful—yet how sweet—her feelings for Scott Lambert had become.

But she was still clueless as to his feelings for *her*. Maybe he only thought of her as a good buddy when he'd needed one last summer. Could there possibly be a future for them . . . together?

Maybe . . . in New York . . . she'd find out.

Maybe . . . in the Big Apple!

Three

Top ten? Oh, wow! I feel like Number One already!

Cissy still had to pinch herself to prove she was really here. She had visited New York twice before—once, as a very young child, when she and her parents had stayed in the Manhattan home of her dad's doctor friend. The home had been gorgeous, but with no children to play with and a lot of elegant "untouchables" sitting around on delicate antiques, she'd been bored to death. The second time was a few years ago when her father attended a medical convention. On that visit, they had stayed in a hotel, never venturing out except for one evening when they took in a Broadway play.

This is different! This is my trip! From the moment Cissy caught sight of the New York skyline from the window of the jet, she was in orbit. After landing at LaGuardia, they sped toward Manhattan in the hotel limousine, the driver whisking them into any available slot in the bumper-to-bumper traffic. But she felt her excitement really skyrocket when the sun began to set over the city. The blue sky blushed hot pink, mirrored in the windows and glass walls of tall buildings that jut-ted into the heavens.

It doesn't get any better than this, she thought as the limo pulled up in front of the Marriott Marquis and she stood for a moment staring at the revolving door that would take her into another world where dreams could come true.

Spellbound, Cissy was hardly aware of Natalie and Scott standing beside her, or the two women—her mom and Aunt Helen—a step behind, as she walked across the threshold into the atrium and paused to take in the sight. Throughout the vaulted lobby, in huge gold planters, stood magnificent Christmas trees, their tiny white lights twinkling like a million stars. Shiny gold bows decorated the trees. Underneath were gaily decorated packages. Flanking the great room, scarlet poinsettias nestled in golden pots, like the treasure at the end of the rainbow.

There was only one word for it—even if the younger crowd *had* worn it out by now. "Awesome!"

She heard her exclamation echoed by Scott and Natalie before the three of them broke the spell of the moment in an explosion of laughter.

The two moms had their own lingo. "Lovely!"

"It's beginning to look a lot like Christmas," Na-talie spoke up, "and it isn't even Thanksgiving yet!"

"Yeah." Scott let out a long sigh. "They must dec-orate early in the Big Apple."

He lifted his camcorder to his shoulder and panned the bustling lobby. Then he motioned them over to the side—Cissy and Natalie in the middle, Cissy's mom and Aunt Helen on either side—where they posed beneath one of the gigantic Christmas trees. He didn't have to coach them on the expression he wanted. Wonder, delight, and anticipation were written all over their faces.

"Registration and elevators on the eighth floor," Elizabeth read from the marquee as soon as Scott turned off the camcorder.

They walked through a corridor and stepped on an escalator to begin the slow ascent. As they rose, mirrored walls reflected a wonderland of glittering lights, balls, bangles, and bells. Somewhere in the background, over the conversations and laughter, Christmas music heralded the season of goodwill. There might be crime in the streets, Cissy thought, but inside these walls, everything was the picture of peace.

She had traveled with her family all her life, had seen Buckingham Palace in London, the Louvre in Paris, and had island-hopped in Hawaii. She had even stayed in a five-star hotel or two. But nothing she had ever done could top this! Here she would not be just a spectator, but a lead player in one of the most thrilling dramas of her life!

A familiar sensation surfaced—that old competitive drive she'd tried so hard to squelch when she turned her life over to Christ. As the escalator climbed toward the eighth floor, she felt herself rising up . . . up . . . up. *Will I be one of the three lucky winners?* she wondered. *Could God possibly have modeling in mind for me as part of His plan?*

That night last spring, when she'd run away with Ron to protest her parents' stand against her going to a New York acting school, she hadn't counted on running *into* a twister that would tangle all her dreams. Thanks to Natalie and this little white dove—she touched the charm dangling from a silver chain around her neck—she'd come to her senses before making the worst mistake of her life! Love and marriage—especially at the wrong time and to the wrong person—were no solution to her problems. Instead, after that tragic night in the storm, she had asked God to help her straighten out the mess she'd made of things. He had led her to apply to a local college and to keep her part-time modeling job at Belk's.

Strange that she was here in New York City, after all. And so far, God hadn't closed any doors.

"This is it," she told the others, stepping out onto the eighth floor and walking over to the registration desk. "I'm Cissy Stiles. I'm here for the Dream Teen model competition."

The desk clerk, a middle-aged New Yorker, looked her over. "I can see why," he mumbled under his breath and punched in her name on his computer. "Models and families are on the thirty-seventh floor." He scrolled the screen and read the data. "You'll be sharing a room with one of the other contestants. The rest of you—your family, I assume—will be staying in an adjoining wing." His manner was matter-of-fact but not unkind—nothing unusual for New Yorkers, so she'd been told. "Your keys." He handed over several flat cards to be inserted into the door locks.

When the other clerks glanced up to stare at Cissy and her entourage, she experienced the first flutter of anxiety. *How am I going to feel when a whole ballroom full of people is giving me the once-over?* She'd know soon enough. But in the meantime, she'd be able to get her bearings before she met with the contest officials in the morning.

Following the directions given by the desk clerk, they found the glass elevators at the end of the hall. Each elevator reminded Natalie of a giant eggbeater, its wire spokes grasping an oval sphere. Crowding into the carpeted cocoon, she noticed that the sides were studded with white lights beneath a brightly lighted golden dome.

"Even the elevators look like decorations," she said, trying not to count the number of floors they were flying past. Looking down, she could see that the atrium lobby seemed to be shrinking to the size of a Christmas card.

Having come up in the service elevator, the bellman was waiting on the hall adjacent to the elevator as they emerged. "Let's get settled in our rooms first," Elizabeth Stiles suggested to Cissy. "Then we'll find yours."

The family suite was located in the rear of the building, on a quiet hallway far removed from the meeting rooms in the front. As the bellman unloaded his luggage cart and carried in the bags, Elizabeth reminded him that they'd be needing a rollaway bed. His sour look was soon replaced with a smile as big as the tip she gave him.

The suite consisted of a large living room with a couch, a coffee table, three large easy chairs flanked by end tables, a counter separating the living room from a compact kitchenette, a bathroom, and a bedroom with adjoining bath. Only one bedroom? Natalie was growing increasingly antsy. Everybody else here was family.

Seeing her skeptical look, Helen Lambert laughed. "Don't worry, Natalie. Elizabeth and I will share the fold-out couch, Scott's rollaway will go in the alcove next to the kitchen, and you can have the bedroom."

"And after the competition, you'll stay in *my* room," Cissy explained.

Natalie forced a smile. For one thing, if Cissy won the contest, hanging out with a high-school student would be the *last* thing she'd want to do. For another, she felt really awful that Cissy's mother and aunt would have to share the couch. But she couldn't very well offer to sleep there herself—not with Scott in the same room. On the other hand . . . "I could take the rollaway, and Scott could have the bedroom."

Scott frowned and put up his hand in a dramatic gesture. "A gentleman would never consent to such a thing."

"And neither would *Scott*," Cissy quipped, giving her cousin a playful shove.

This time Natalie felt herself relaxing as the laughter erupted.

"It's only for three nights," Mrs. Stiles assured her. "Besides, the couch opens up into a queen-sized bed, which is about three times larger than the one Helen and I had when we were girls." She smiled at her younger sister. "We used to snuggle together whenever there was a storm or something went bump in the night."

"I ended up in your bed a lot, didn't I, Elizabeth?"

Helen asked affectionately. "Especially after Mama and Dad died."

Before some gloomy memory could spoil the festive mood, Cissy broke in. "Let's go take a look at your room, Nat."

Natalie followed Cissy into the spacious bedroom, set her bag on the luggage rack, and crossed the plush carpet to the window wall. "Can you believe this?"

A forest of tall towers loomed directly in front of them, and antlike figures scurried on the sidewalks thirty-seven stories below. Off to the far right, barely visible in the twilight, was a ribbon of water.

"That, my friend, is the East River," Cissy pointed out with the assurance of a veteran traveler. "Now, let's go see if *I* have a riverfront view. I'm dying to meet my roommate . . . that is, if she came a day early like I did."

Scott was putting a blank tape in his camcorder when they entered the living room. "Oh, I'll want some shots of the models, too, Scott," Cissy spoke up. "Why don't you come along with Natalie and me now—if it's okay with you, Mom." She glanced at her mother and her Aunt Helen, who were checking out the kitchen.

Without waiting for a reply, Cissy picked up her overnight case and started for the door.

"Just don't get too wrapped up in that fantasy world of yours, Cissy," Elizabeth cautioned. "I'll want to see your room, meet your roommate and the chaperone. . . ."

"Sure, Mom," Cissy said on the way out the door. "There will be plenty of time for that. See you later."

But this is no fantasy world, she was thinking. *This is for real!*

Her room—one of many to the left of the hallway—was almost opposite her mom's suite, near the meeting rooms where the models would convene in the morning. On the right, a railing, roped with Christmas greenery and twinkling with lights, protected the open area that extended all the way from the first floor to the forty-eighth.

"It's a long way down," Natalie observed, peering at the atrium.

"It'd make a great little jumping-off place." Scott's remark wasn't very funny, and they laughed nervously. "Don't even think I'll try for a shot of the lobby from here."

Scott didn't linger long, but caught up with Cissy and Natalie. "Hey, this is quite a hike. What's your room number, cuz?"

Cissy pulled her key card from the pocket of her jacket. "It's 3715 . . . right about *here.*" She came to a stop in front of an elegant doorway with a brass knocker.

"Hey, you two turn around, and I'll get a shot of you in front of your room," Scott directed with a twirling motion of his hand.

Cissy set her overnight case next to the wall, reached for Natalie's arm, and turned to face Scott, a million-watt smile in place.

Just then, a guy backed out of the meeting room with his camcorder on his shoulder. As Scott yelled, "Watch out!" the fellow tripped over Cissy's overnight case. He grasped the doorknob to steady himself, his camcorder swinging around and striking Cissy in the head.

It all happened so fast that Scott—camera still rolling—had only an impression of flailing elbows and thrashing legs. He could see his cousin making a grab for Natalie, then the two girls going down in a heap on the floor, the photographer piling in on top, his camcorder bouncing off the carpet.

When they untangled themselves and came up for air, only Cissy—holding her hand to her head—was moaning softly. When she pulled her hand away, there was a bright red stain on her palm. "I'm bleeding!"

Still on her knees, Natalie helped Cissy lean against the wall. Zipping open the makeup bag, she found a tissue and pressed it on the wound, just above Cissy's left eye.

"You klutz!" Scott flared at the guy, who seemed more interested in retrieving his precious camcorder than anything else. "Why couldn't you watch where you were going?"

"Hey, I'm sorry," the guy mumbled, still fumbling for the pieces of his camera. "Anything I can do?"

"You've already done it, buddy! You've probably blown my cousin's chances of winning the model competition!"

The guy, who appeared to be a few years older than Scott, raised a dark eyebrow. "Your cousin is a finalist?"

"That's right," Scott replied, his camcorder still whirring.

The young man waved helplessly at the camera, then turned toward Cissy. But his apologies fell on deaf ears.

"My head! I'm bleeding!" she wailed, her volume increasing by the minute.

By this time, several other girls had appeared at the meeting-room doorway to see what all the commotion was about. From behind them, a woman rushed out, her silvery gray hair framing a concerned face, her dark eyes taking in the spectacle on the floor. "Antonio, what happened?"

"She's one of the models in the competition," he explained to the woman, who knelt in front of Cissy.

"I'm Jane Sansone, a chaperone." After a quick appraisal, she helped Cissy to her feet. "Let's get you inside, dear, where you can be more comfortable."

Natalie picked up Cissy's key card that had fallen on the floor in the scuffle, inserted the card in the door slot, and unlocked it. With her arm around Cissy, the woman led her into the room, followed by Natalie and a young girl with lush auburn hair hanging to her waist.

Still muttering under his breath, the photographer scrambled around for the broken pieces of his equipment and cradled them in his hands like a baby. Scott's camcorder continued to grind away. "Just my luck to have this little fiasco recorded for all the world to see," the guy grumbled, getting to his feet. Holding the remains of his camera against him with one hand, he dusted off his pants with the other, then glanced over at the open door, where several girls now gathered, craning their necks to see what was going on.

Only then did Scott turn off his camcorder and go in to check on Cissy.

She was lying on one of the twin beds with her eyes closed, a damp cloth draped over her forehead. Natalie was sitting on the edge of the bed, gently stroking her hand, while the auburn-haired girl perched on the other bed, all hair and huge green eyes in a pale oval face.

"Antonio," Jane Sansone called through the doorway, "please come in here and call the hotel doctor. He needs to take a look at this." She continued to apply pressure to the wound. "Antonio is the son of the modeling agency's owners," she explained. "I'm sure the Carlos will want to take care of any expenses."

Scott stepped aside to let the tall guy through the door, then watched him pick up the phone on the kitchen counter and dial a single digit. When he finished, he nodded and hung up. "The doctor will be right up."

Scott glared at him. In fact, every eye in the room— except Cissy's—was riveted on this Antonio. It was all his fault!

Jane Sansone broke the uncomfortable silence. "Is her family here?"

"I could go get her mom," Natalie offered.

But Scott, still standing in the doorway, shook his head. "I'll go."

"Maybe I should go with him," the Italian guy said, but he didn't seem too keen on the idea.

But Ms. Sansone gave him a withering glance. "That's *exactly* what you should do."

Antonio tried apologizing again when Scott broke

the news about Cissy's accident to his mom and Aunt Liz when they reached the suite. But there was no time for introductions or explanations. They seemed oblivious to anything but finding out how badly Cissy was hurt.

When they reached the opposite side of the building, they all assumed—correctly—that the man carrying a black bag and striding up the hall ahead of them was the doctor.

"This must be our patient," the balding man said, hurrying into Cissy's hotel room. "What happened?"

There was a moment of silence before Antonio spoke up. "I bumped into her and my camera struck her head. Pretty hard, I guess." He grimaced and glanced at Scott, who was fiddling with his camera again. "I'm sure *he* has all the evidence right there in living color."

Surprised at his sarcasm, Scott looked over at him quickly. Just as abruptly, Antonio turned his head away. Weird, Scott thought, how familiar that action seemed. Just like his mom—when she'd been disgusted with herself after a drinking bout. Later, he'd learned it was guilt that had caused her to act that way.

"Hey, Antonio," Scott said under his breath so the others wouldn't hear. "If it'll make you feel any better, I know it was an accident."

Now it was Antonio's turn to look surprised. Instantly he lost his defensive attitude and murmured, "Thanks."

As the doctor sat beside Cissy's bed and leaned over to examine the cut, Jane shooed Scott and Antonio out. "Why don't you two wait out in the hall?"

Outside Cissy's room, Antonio picked up the biggest piece of the damaged camera. "Man! A photographer without any equipment!"

"I'll be glad to take a look and see if there's anything I can do," Scott volunteered.

The guy's defense mechanism kicked in again. "Believe me, there isn't. I'm not exactly an amateur." Antonio gave a short laugh, curling his lip. "Or maybe I *am*. A real pro doesn't back into people with his camera in his hand."

Scott grinned. "I've dropped mine before, and I didn't have an excuse, like stumbling over a bag."

"Well, it wouldn't be so bad if I weren't on assignment." Antonio raked his hand through his thick black waves. "I'm gonna get skinned!"

"Didn't the chaperone say your parents own the modeling agency?"

"Yeah, but that only makes it worse. They'll show no mercy!" Antonio groaned. "I'm supposed to be taking informal shots of the models before the official event begins tomorrow. But when my folks find out about this, I'm dead meat."

It didn't take Scott long to hit on the right thing to do. "Till then, would you like to use my camcorder?"

There was a look of stunned disbelief on the guy's face. "You mean it?"

"Sure." Scott shrugged. "If you need it for your job, be my guest. Besides, I brought my still camera, too."

Antonio squinted, sizing him up. "You look a little young to be in this line of work."

"I'm seventeen." Scott blushed, feeling like a kid.

"Photography is a hobby right now, but I hope to be a professional someday. In fact, one of the reasons I'm here—besides cheering my cousin on—is to check out some schools."

For the first time, Antonio's tense jaw relaxed. "Maybe I can help you out there. I graduated from college last spring and am in training at the agency. Uh . . . if you're really serious about letting me use your camera . . . you'd take out that incriminating video, wouldn't you?"

Scott grinned. "Yeah. I'll save it for the tabloids." He opened the case, removed the tape and pocketed it, then snapped the case shut. "Here you go." He handed over the camcorder.

Antonio nodded, his mouth twisting in a wry smile. "Thanks. You're going to be around for a while?"

"A lot depends on what happens with the competition, of course. But either way, we plan to stick around a few days to take in the sights."

"Great! I'll be pretty busy until after the competition. Then we'll get together on this." He stuck out his hand.

Scott took it in a firm handshake that made him feel like Antonio's equal. He released his grip when his mother and Natalie came out of Cissy's room, then turned and made the introductions.

"The doctor thinks Cissy should be X-rayed, just to be on the safe side," his mom told them. "It's not a deep cut, but she'll probably need stitches."

"Mrs. Lambert, I'm really sorry about all this. Is there anything I can do? Drive her to the hospital?"

"Thank you, but the doctor has already made arrangements for her to take a hotel limo."

Antonio sighed. "Well, I doubt if she'd welcome *my* company right now anyway."

"Scott," his mother said, "Elizabeth and the chaperone will go with Cissy. I'll stay here with you two. There's no need for you to spend the evening in a hospital waiting room."

Natalie wasn't sure if she should follow Helen back to the suite, or wait for Scott, who seemed to have struck up a friendship with the photographer.

Just then a bell shrilled, and the tall Italian whipped out a cellular phone and flipped open the case. "Thanks. I'll be ready." He refolded the phone and looked at Scott. "The desk clerk says another model is on her way up." He patted the camcorder. "Thanks, pal. I won't forget this."

Natalie wasn't sure what that was all about, but her awkward feeling melted—along with her heart—the minute Scott walked over and smiled. "Sorry about all this, Nat."

"Oh, it's not *your* fault."

"I just hope this vacation doesn't turn out like the one at Lake Oakwood." His tone was grim as they made their way down the hall toward the suite. "Katlyn's still got the scars to remember it by."

Katlyn! She wasn't even here, but Scott was thinking about her! Natalie felt a sinking sensation in the pit of her stomach—like the dip in the roller-coaster ride at Fair Park. This was going to turn out to be a memorable trip, all right—but with all the *wrong* memories.

Cissy pressed the cool washcloth over her eye and against the bone as the doctor had directed. For a minor cut, it had sure bled a lot. Her head hurt, she felt dizzy, and her vision was blurred from trying to see through one squinted eye.

She leaned back against the metal wall of the service elevator. No bright lights this time, but she felt her hopes plummet along with the elevator—all the way to the first floor and out the back door at ground level, where the limo was waiting at the curb.

Cissy exited, her mom on one side and Jane Sansone on the other, into a dingy street filled with smelly exhaust fumes. The odor made her nauseous, and the honking of horns drove the pain through her skull like a jackhammer. With no dinner and having lost all that blood, she was feeling pretty woozy.

On the way to the hospital, she tried very hard to believe that everything was going to be all right. But as much as she tried to ignore them, a swarm of nagging questions kept playing in her mind. *Why did this have to happen to me? Is God trying to tell me I should drop out of the competition?*

And if I don't . . . what else could happen?

Four

By the time Cissy was back from the hospital emergency room, she'd made up her mind to stick it out. Depending, of course, upon whether she'd be fit to compete when the time came.

I'm no quitter. Besides, God surely wouldn't have brought me here if He hadn't had some plan in mind.

While she was waiting for Jane Sansone to order sandwiches from room service, Cissy checked out her wound in her hand mirror. Fortunately, the cut was right on the bone, and the doctor had stitched as close to her eyebrow as possible. However, the area above her eye was swollen and red. "Some discoloration is to be expected by morning," he'd said. "But you're a lucky young woman. If that cut had been a quarter of an inch lower. . . ." She shuddered, considering.

"Oh, you're back," called a voice from the adjoining room, where the door had been propped open.

The long-haired girl stepped in, followed by two other girls and a petite woman with a decidedly Asian cast to her features. Jane Sansone introduced the woman first. "This is Min Collins, who works with me in the makeup department of the agency." Turning to a brunette with unusual gray-green eyes, she went on, "And this is Nan, who comes from the ranch country of Montana, and Heather, from Indiana."

Cissy was thinking that the Indiana girl, with her mousy brown hair and eyes, looked like an unlikely candidate for a national contest—until she smiled. Then her face took on a pixieish quality, with dimples denting both cheeks.

At fifteen and sixteen, both girls were younger than she. But when the auburn-haired girl pushed her lush mane behind her shoulders, her face appeared incredibly young, Cissy thought—probably about Amy's age. "We've sorta met already . . . when you first got hurt," she said. "I'm Selena Raintree, your roommate . . . and I'm from Georgia—the southern part, that is."

There was a ripple of laughter. With that drawl, there was no mistaking her southern roots. "I'm sure glad you're not hurt real bad."

"Thanks. And you're right. I suppose it could have been worse."

Jane answered the knock at the door, and a waiter wheeled in a service cart. The girls jumped up to leave, but Cissy motioned them back to their seats on the twin bed opposite hers. "It's all right. You can stay."

While Cissy ate her sandwich, Selena leaned closer to get a better look at the bandaged forehead. "When I saw all that blood, I thought you were a goner. But that lump's not too bad."

Cissy smiled at the girl's look of concern. "The doctor said most of the swelling would probably be gone by morning."

"Well, I don't know how you can be so calm." Nan

folded her legs under her on the bed. "I think you're being really brave."

"Yeah," Heather agreed. "How awful to have something like this happen. Especially now!"

To her own surprise, Cissy shrugged it off. "Modeling and acting used to be the most important things in my life. But now . . . well . . . if God doesn't want me to win, then that just means He has something better for me."

From the stunned looks on their faces and the awkward silence, Cissy suspected they didn't understand. Just a few months ago, neither would she! She picked up her sandwich again, and the others changed the subject, chattering about what they planned to wear to the meeting the next morning.

"Am I the oldest one in the competition?" Cissy asked Jane, after Nan and Heather had left for their room. "Eighteen suddenly sounds ancient!"

"There's one other girl just a few months younger than you," Jane told her, gathering up the remains of her own sandwich. "Most are fifteen and sixteen, though. There's one thirteen-year-old, and Selena here is the next youngest. Roommates are assigned alphabetically, not by age."

"In some beauty contests, they do that for a reason," Selena spoke up. "They want to know how each contestant relates to people of different ages and nationalities." She glanced over at their chaperone, who was unpacking her pajamas. "Right, Jane?"

"Now, Selena," Jane chided. "I told you earlier that I can't say how or why the agency makes its decisions." She went into the bathroom and closed the door.

Selena grinned. But she didn't speak again until she heard the sound of the shower running. "I think you and I will be two of the winners."

"Are you kidding?" Cissy flinched, feeling a stab of pain shooting through her forehead. She reached up to touch the bandage. "What kind of chance do I have in *this* condition?"

"Oh, believe me, you'll get a lot of mileage out of this." Selena spoke with the voice of authority. She might be young, Cissy thought, but she had spunk. "Everybody will feel sorry for you. And the photographer who did it is the son of the agency owners—"

"Selena!" Cissy interrupted. "I wouldn't want to win for *that* reason."

"Oh, that's not the main reason," she went on with a wave of her hand. "The main reason is because you're a Christian. That's why I think I'll win, too. I always pray before my competitions, and I've never lost one yet. My mom started me out when I was just a baby. I have twenty-three . . . no, twenty-four trophies and ribbons." She smiled. "It's just great being on God's side, isn't it?"

Cissy nodded, giving her a sidelong look. "It's the best place to be," she agreed. "But sometimes God surprises us. I haven't been a Christian very long, but I've learned that my ideas don't often turn out to be God's ideas. Just last spring, I thought my boyfriend was the answer to all my problems. But he wasn't right for me at all."

Selena practically glowed. "See? If you'd gotten married, you couldn't have been in the competition!"

"Right, but that doesn't guarantee I'll win. Especially now."

"Oh, I just *feel* it!" Selena propped up her knees on the bed and hugged them to her.

How quickly things changed, Cissy thought to herself. When she'd arrived this afternoon, she'd never felt so confident. Now, it was as if she'd done an about-face. Oh, not that her faith had been particularly damaged by the accident. But she knew—better than most—that it hadn't been her successes that had brought her closer to God . . . but her failures.

Still, when the lights were out and she lay awake long after Selena was sound asleep, Cissy wondered, *Would I be as brave or as positive if the cut had been worse? Or if the camera had hit me in my eye instead of above it? And can I truly chalk this competition up to experience and accept it graciously . . . if I don't win?*

By morning, Cissy feared she had the answer to her questions of the night before. At the first shrill ring of the phone, she was wide awake, and while Jane was talking, she reached for the hand mirror on the bedside table.

"Sorry," Jane frowned over the mouthpiece—"but there will be no interviews until 11:00." She hesitated, looking surprised as she listened. "No, it was only a little cut. She'll be fine."

Jane hung up, shaking her head. "Now, how did that reporter get wind of this?" Still in her robe, she padded back into the bathroom to brush her teeth.

"Great!" gushed Selena, glancing at Cissy in the dresser mirror and beginning to unwind her hair from huge hot rollers. "With all this attention, you're bound to win!"

"Does that mean black eyes and grotesque features are in?" Cissy rebutted, sitting up and turning her face toward Selena. Beneath her eye was a purplish quarter-moon bruise. Without the bandage, the red-streaked lump was smaller than the night before, but plainly visible beneath the black stitches puckering the skin and lifting her eyebrow at an unnatural angle.

Selena gasped, obviously shocked at Cissy's appearance. "Maybe . . . maybe you can cover it," she said weakly.

"Makeup will never cover this!" Cissy wailed, thrusting the hand mirror aside. "*Now* what am I going to do?" She slumped back onto the pillow. "Mom says I ought to be thankful I don't have a concussion."

"Well, it's a tough break, all right," Selena admitted, beginning to brush her mass of thick auburn hair.

Cissy thought the younger girl's green eyes brightened. Even as a Christian, Selena had to be human enough to know that her own chances of winning would be greater with Cissy out of the running.

"Remember, I work in the makeup department," Jane reminded them, coming in from the bathroom just as the phone rang again. "Hello? Yes . . . I'll ask." She covered the mouthpiece. "Cissy, Antonio Carlo would like to speak with you."

Antonio Carlo? The guy who caused this whole fiasco? "No way," she muttered under her breath, getting up to try to do something about her face.

"He just wants to apologize," Jane said when she had hung up.

"He'll just have to wait!" Cissy snapped and glanced at Selena, who looked sympathetic. That's how everybody would view her now . . . that is, if they could stand to look at her at all.

With Selena taking her turn in the bathroom, Cissy sat at the dressing table to take stock. Her blond hair was too short to wear over one side of her face. And even with Jane's trained hand, the concealer didn't cover the strange tilt of her eyebrow. She couldn't win with half a face!

"I look like Dr. Jekyll and Mr. Hyde—or *Miss Hideous* is more like it!" Cissy groaned after they'd done all they could do to patch her up.

Until now, she hadn't realized just how much she'd wanted to win—to compete anyway. She hadn't planned to lose by default. Certainly not *the fault* of Antonio Carlo!

The clumsy jerk. Maybe she *should* talk to him, tell him—

She groaned again as the phone rang and a knock came at the door simultaneously.

"Selena, will you get the door?" Jane asked as she reached for the phone, then handed it to Cissy. "It's your mother."

"Mom? Oh, don't worry. I'm fine." Had she really said that? Maybe her acting ability would come in handy. Maybe if she kept telling herself all was well, she could regain the confidence of the night before. "Tell Nat and Scott hello. Aunt Helen, too. See ya later."

She hung up and turned to see Selena cradling a bouquet of flowers that had just been delivered. "Yum. Roses." The girl's auburn hair swung forward as she bent her head to breathe in the fragrance of the deep red half-opened buds wrapped in tissue paper. "For

Miss Cissy Stiles, the guy said."

"For me? But why would anyone be sending *me* flowers? Oh"—Cissy gave a short laugh—"it's probably my consolation prize . . . from my family." What else could she do? She might as well make a joke of the whole disaster. She took out the card, read it, and thrust it toward Jane.

"Please accept this peace offering as a token of my deepest regret," Jane read aloud. "I'll be in the meeting room next door at 9:30 to apologize in person. I need your forgiveness, lest I fling myself from the nearest bridge."

This time Cissy smiled. She had to admit that she was amused and more than a little curious. After all, she'd never laid eyes on the guy. She didn't even know what Antonio Carlo looked like. But he sounded like he had a sense of humor. "Um, where *is* the nearest bridge?"

Jane grinned. "Don't worry. Antonio will survive. But he doesn't give up easily. So you might as well see him."

<hr />

By 9:15, Cissy had had her breakfast and was dressed in a dark red wool suit that did wonders for her figure. *Best not to call attention to my face,* she thought with a wry grimace.

Feeling a clump of mascara underneath one eye, she took a last look in the mirror. Careful not to get makeup in the wound, Jane had covered it with a tiny flesh-colored Band-Aid before applying the concealer.

"Hmph!" Cissy snorted under her breath. "I just

hope I can conceal my disgust when I meet this Mr. Carlo!"

What about forgiveness? whispered an unfamiliar small voice on the inside. Guiltily, she glanced at the roses Jane was arranging in a vase on the counter. *And what about responsibility?* whispered another voice. *Antonio Carlo needs to be aware of the seriousness of his actions. He could have blinded you!*

"Yeah!" Cissy spoke aloud. "He could have *blinded* me!"

Selena, who was doing her nails, looked up in surprise.

Cissy glanced at her watch. It was 9:25—more than half an hour before the other models would convene in the hospitality suite. "I've decided to see Antonio Carlo and get it over with," she said with determination. Better still, he needed to see *her*—see the damage he'd done with his carelessness.

Jane shrugged. "Fine. It's up to you. But I'll need to go with you. Selena, I'll open the connecting door so you won't be alone."

On her way next door to the meeting room, Cissy lectured herself. *Maybe if I keep up a brave front and keep on saying, 'God's will, not mine' often enough, I'll really begin to mean it.*

Taking a deep breath, she went in.

He was standing across the room, looking out the window. From the back, he seemed younger than she'd expected. He was wearing gray slacks and an expensive-looking sweater that molded the muscles rippling across his broad shoulders. Thick, well-groomed hair curled at his collar. *Wonderful!* she thought with more than a trace of sarcasm. *He probably looks terrific, while I look like something that was run over by a freight train!*

"Antonio," Jane called, closing the door behind them, leaving the three of them alone in the room.

Cissy was on the verge of telling the big jerk what she thought of him—his clumsiness, his stupidity for backing into a hallway and swinging his heavy camera around without looking—when he turned and gazed at her with the most incredibly warm, expressive brown eyes she'd ever seen!

Oh, wow! The icicle in her good eye melted like a popsicle on a hot day—like an ice cream cone in the sun—like butter in the microwave. Feeling faint, she walked to the nearest chair and sat down.

The next thing she knew, he was on his knees, apologizing, begging her forgiveness, and vowing to do his best to make this up to her. He took her hand like some gallant knight from King Arthur's legendary court. But when she remembered that this was the guy who had ruined her best chance at a fabulous career, she snatched it back.

Looking crushed, he got to his feet and stood staring down at her. "You have every reason to despise me," he said contritely with a trace of an accent. He ran his hand through his hair, the deep waves springing back to curl over his forehead. He looked just like a bad little boy who'd been called to the principal's office.

Her silent lecture began all over again. *Control yourself, Cissy Stiles! It doesn't matter how handsome and charming he is. Besides, he's probably just an actor . . . well, so are you. I just hope you can act unimpressed. Don't you dare let him suspect you could fall for someone like him!*

He took the chair beside her. Fortunately, it was on her "good" side.

"I am truly sorry," he went on. "If you don't forgive me, I'm going to kill myself . . . or at the very least—" he got serious—"I could lose my job."

"Well . . ." She felt herself melting again and stiffened her shoulders. "You probably made me lose mine . . . at least, my future job. Because of my eye, I may not even be allowed to compete. This modeling contest could have led to a whole new career for me."

"I know that. And you can't imagine how bad I feel. . . ." He dropped his head for a moment, then looked up with a mischievous grin. "But I do have another little peace offering."

"A new eye?"

"Something *for* the eye."

This guy knew all the great lines in history. But he was pretty convincing. She went along. "No steak, please. I don't need to smell like a cow on top of everything else."

"You smell like . . . mmmph!" He kissed his fingers and flung a gesture into the air. "Like . . . heaven."

"You've been there?"

"Not before I met you."

Cissy had to laugh. "*That* was heaven? Well, save me from the other place!" She glanced over at Jane on the other side of the room, grateful she was there. Jane was grinning like the Cheshire Cat from *Alice in Wonderland*.

Antonio pulled a small white leather case from his back pocket and handed it to Cissy.

She opened it and drew out a pair of tinted designer

sunglasses and lifted them for Jane to see. "Sunglasses!" At least she could cover her wounded eye in style.

She was turning to thank Antonio at the very same moment he leaned toward her. She blinked, feeling the glob of mascara on her bottom lash. He was so close she could make out a faint five o'clock shadow, a flash of perfect white teeth—and those velvety eyes, laughing into hers.

He took the words right out of her mouth. "You have the most fabulous eyes I've ever seen!"

"Me—I?" Cissy stammered. "With this shiner?"

"Can you ever forgive me?"

She couldn't move, could barely breathe. Maybe it was the injury that made her dizzy. But she doubted it. "I . . . I'm sure I'll be okay."

"We won't take any chances. Let's try the glasses."

He helped her up—it wasn't just the high heels . . . or her injury . . . that made her unsteady on her feet—and over to a wall mirror, where Cissy carefully fitted the glasses over her eyes.

"Hmmm. I wouldn't have believed anyone could be more enchanting. But I think the glasses add to your mystique."

She couldn't help but laugh, even though she didn't believe a word the guy was saying. Still, she had to admit, the glasses *did* hide the worst of the damage.

"I'm not allowed to fraternize with the models until after the competition," he said, "but I'm not going to let you out of my sight . . . until I know you're as perfect as you look!"

Five

Natalie sat on the couch in the hospitality suite, sipping an orange juice, while she waited for Scott, who had overslept. From here, she had a great view of the whole room. Helen Lambert and Elizabeth Stiles, talking with Maria and Tomas Carlo, the owners of the Top Ten Modeling Agency, who had insisted on apologizing personally for the terrible accident the night before. The models, as they filed into the room in groups or two by two. Cissy, in deep conversation with that good-looking Antonio guy. . . .

Cissy looked terrific herself, Natalie thought, in a red suit with black piping on the collar and cuffs. Her blond hair shone like corn silks in a sunny field, and the dark glasses she was wearing made her look like a movie star walking onto the set. If no one knew, they'd never suspect she had a black eye.

Looking down at her own outfit, Natalie realized she probably should have dressed up a little more. She'd worn her new black pants with a long-sleeved T-shirt under her black quilted jacket. Cissy had said she couldn't go wrong with basic black. But Natalie had failed to ask Cissy about shirts with religious sayings like the one she sported.

Well, there was no sense in sitting here like a knot on a log. Just as she was getting up to go find Scott, Natalie spotted him coming in the door. Instead of looking for her, though, he made a beeline for Antonio—to talk photography probably. Yep, just as she thought. Scott was showing him how to load his video-cam.

Natalie was beginning to feel completely unnecessary when she noticed a young woman bustling around in the kitchenette of the meeting room. The very pregnant woman was measuring out coffee in a big urn. The coffeepot began to perk and growl as she arranged napkins, spoons, creamer, and a sugar container on a silver tray. Natalie remembered something her mom had said—that all pregnant women had a kind of glow about them. Maybe it was a reflection of her pretty pink dress ballooning over the small miracle growing inside her or a flush from the heat, but the woman had that glow. And the expression on the face—unlike those of some people up here—was friendly.

Natalie took a chance and walked around the partition into the kitchen. "Anything I can do to help?"

The woman looked up, flustered. "Oh, I couldn't let you do that. You're a guest—" she looked again— "or maybe a model."

Natalie hooted. "Not me! I'm just here with a friend. Please . . . you'd be doing me a favor. I need something to do."

"Well, since you put it that way, I *could* use a bathroom break—bad!" The woman patted her tummy.

"I'm Beth—and this is Bethanne. We're *both* grateful! Be right back."

While she was away, Natalie took off her jacket. She was pouring orange juice when a couple of models walked up. One was a Latino beauty with her dark hair slicked back into a twist. The other looked like a Japanese doll Rose had once—with a cap of short black hair and bangs framing delicate features. But there was something about the eyes. She looked sad. Or frightened. Well, who *wouldn't* be scared—competing in a national contest!

But before Natalie could think much more about it, a third model—a tall African-American who reminded her of Twila—hurtled through the door and over to the counter with all the zest of a cyclone. She stuck out her hand. "Hi! I'm Ardath!"

Nothing shy about this girl, Natalie thought. Even at her own height of five feet seven inches, Natalie was a good five inches shorter.

"And this is Kameko and Courtney. We'll pass on the coffee and juice. But would you have some of that bottled water?"

"I . . . I don't really know. I'll look." Natalie was searching the fridge when Beth bounced back.

"Perrier's in the door. Here you go." She popped the tops and handed over three bottles. As the girls strolled away, Beth sighed. "Boy, you saved my life! This is my first baby, and I had no idea how it would be."

Her gaze dropped to the front of Natalie's shirt. " 'Jesus Is the Reason for the Season,' " she read aloud. "Huh . . . I hadn't thought much about that since I was a kid. Our family never did go to church much, but now that I'm gonna have a kid of my own, I want to be sure *she* goes."

Natalie nodded. "Mom says baby books are okay, but the Bible is the biggest help in raising children. She has four."

Beth lifted a brow. "Bibles . . . or children?"

They giggled together and fell into an easy conversation. For the first time this morning, Natalie was glad she'd worn her "talking T-shirt" as her mom called it. You just never knew when you might get an opportunity to say something that would help.

Then Mr. Carlo was speaking into a microphone, instructing the models to find a seat. Natalie felt out of place again. She ought to get out of here. If she could just find Scott. . . .

"So here you are, dear." It was Mrs. Stiles, speaking in a whisper, while Tomas Carlo launched the first session. "Helen and I were wondering what had happened to you."

Before Natalie could get a word in edgewise, Helen spoke up. "Well, wouldn't you know she'd be pitching in to help somewhere."

"Where's Scott?" Natalie asked when they were outside the meeting rooms.

"The Carlo boy asked him to stay around for a while and help with the videotaping." Helen gave an airy wave of her hand as they walked down the hallway toward their rooms. "Don't worry. He'll meet us for lunch. Now let's go look at the brochures we collected and plan what we want to see after the competition."

When Scott rushed in over an hour later, he wasn't thinking of food. Or of Natalie, either, she thought miserably.

"Mom, Antonio has asked me if I'd like to check out the agency. He wants to get some shots of the models when they stop in after lunch, and he asked me to help him set up."

"But you haven't eaten—" Helen Lambert protested.

"We'll grab a bite on the way." He really sounded gung ho to be off.

"Not to mention the fact that you have a guest, son. . . ."

Scott ducked his head a little and shot Natalie a sheepish glance. "Hey, I don't want you guys to feel I'm leaving you in the lurch. Are you okay with this, Nat?"

A wave of regret washed over her, but she really couldn't be selfish. Antonio could be very important to Scott's future. Fortunately, she managed to keep her disappointment to herself. "Sure, Scott. Go ahead."

Helen stepped up and put a consoling arm around Natalie. "After lunch, we'll check out the hotel gift shops. We hadn't really planned to sight see until after the competition anyway."

Natalie could tell that Scott was pretty relieved.

"I'll be home long before dinnertime," he promised, jumping up to grab his still camera. " 'Bye Nat."

" 'Bye," she called after him. But he'd already bolted from the room.

A short while later, Natalie was sitting in one of the hotel restaurants with the two women. Both Helen Lambert and Elizabeth Stiles were doing everything possible to include her in their conversation. But they succeeded only in making her feel yuckier than ever. She nodded politely but kept sipping her iced tea, hoping to force down the lump in her throat.

"I don't know what we would have done without you, Natalie," Scott's aunt was saying. "Cissy might have been seriously hurt—or worse—the night she ran away with Ron. But you were there just when she needed someone." She looked embarrassed and twirled her teaspoon. "Too bad her own mother couldn't get through to her."

"Well, what about *me*, Elizabeth?" Helen Lambert spoke up. "My batting average isn't so good, either. I might never have gotten up the courage to give up my drinking . . . and Zac—well, will we ever forget that awful night with Katlyn?"

If there was anything Natalie wanted to forget right now, it was Katlyn Chander. But she kept popping up—even way up here in New York City.

Not that Natalie hadn't been happy to share her faith with Cissy and Zac—and she was honestly glad Katlyn was recovering so well. But she didn't need an hourly reminder of the one girl who could ruin this trip for her!

What am I doing here anyway? Natalie wondered. She'd served her purpose with the Stileses and the Lamberts. But that was then, and this was now.

At least Scott was a model son. His folks sure had no complaints there. Oh, he might have had some problems in the past, but he'd gotten that all straightened out. He was smart, mature, and gorgeous—and he had goals! He really had it all together—especially now that he'd become part of the youth group at church. *He* certainly didn't need her. That was becoming more and more obvious.

Nope. Natalie was beginning to think she'd made a big mistake in tagging along on Cissy's dream.

After lunch, the women browsed through several shops and Natalie picked up a few souvenirs to take back home. Her sisters—particularly Amy and Rose—would go wild over something from the Big Apple.

She was looking over the small items in her bedroom around five o'clock when Scott tapped on the door.

"Hey, Nat, would you come out here? I have something to ask you."

"Sure," she called, doing her best to work up some enthusiasm. She wasn't ready for another letdown. In fact, she'd prayed that afternoon that she'd be able to recapture her old optimism—and not just the Christmas spirit, either. It was a whole lot more than that, and she knew it. She needed God's Spirit to help her quit feeling sorry for herself and to think about the others.

She dragged herself into the sitting area, half expecting to hear that Antonio Carlo had offered Scott a partnership in the business or something. But what he had to say was even more mind-blowing.

"How about dinner tonight, Nat? Just the two of

us." He didn't take his eyes off Natalie, and she could feel her heart hammering like crazy. "That is, if it's okay with you, Mom."

"Oh, Scott"—Helen Lambert's voice was strained—"it's not safe for two young people to be out alone in New York."

"Mom," he began, and Natalie thought he had never sounded so grown-up, "I want to make it up to Natalie for spending the whole afternoon with Antonio. So I thought she might enjoy The View."

It took a minute for Scott's meaning to sink in. "Oh, you mean the hotel's rooftop restaurant." Mrs. Lambert seemed relieved, then gave a little laugh. "But, son, you couldn't possibly get reservations this late on Thanksgiving Eve."

He gave his mother a big grin. "I got lucky. I called this afternoon from the agency and found out they'd just had a cancellation. We can have a table at 6:30, as long as we're out by eight. Okay, Nat?"

"That sounds wonderful, Scott. I'd love to."

"Think you two will have time to see the six o'clock news?" Cissy's mom put in. "The media was to meet with the models this morning, so they might be on."

Scott cut his eyes around at Natalie. "I can change in no time. What about you?"

"I'll go get ready now. Just call me when the news comes on. I wouldn't want to miss anything." Natalie hurried toward her room, hardly able to believe it. This wasn't the prom, but Scott had actually asked her for a real date! And all afternoon, she'd been thinking he was so caught up in his photography and all those gorgeous models that he hadn't given her a thought!

She ran to the closet and looked through the clothes Cissy had helped her pick out. Winter white was just as basic as black, so Cissy had told her. She decided on the ivory satin skirt and blouse and laid it out on the bed, then showered and shampooed.

Dressing quickly, she dried her hair and brushed it to one side—the way Scott liked it. At least he'd seemed to like it that one time she'd tried the style at the lake. She was just fastening tiny gold hoop earrings when Helen Lambert called through the door.

"News in five minutes, Natalie."

Taking one last look in the mirror, she noticed her White Dove pin lying on the dresser and pinned it on the lapel of her blouse. The white wings blended with the ivory satin, but the tiny rhinestone that formed the eye winked back at her reflection. For a second, the thought of Ruthie's parting shot came to mind: "Better wear your pin and leave it unclasped—in case he tries to get too close!"

She was smiling at the thought of her adorable harebrained friend when she entered the sitting room.

"Wow, Nat! You look great!" Scott exclaimed.

Her heart did flip-flops. "You don't look so bad yourself." She didn't dare say what she really thought—that in those dark pants and light blue band-collar shirt, he was drop-dead gorgeous!

A fleeting thought dropped into her mind like a rock. *How do you think you're going to compete with all those models?* It was an ugly little thought, and for an instant she felt like backing out. She thought she'd come to terms with her wholesome, all-American look a long time ago, but being with with all those beauty contest winners this morning had made her feel like plain vanilla in a roomful of hot fudge sundaes. *And don't think those other girls don't know it!* the little voice taunted. *Some of them were practically drooling all over Scott this morning.*

Well, they couldn't have him. He'd asked *her* to dinner—not the beauty finalists. And she intended to enjoy every minute of it.

Elizabeth turned up the volume on the TV just as the newscast came on. "At the top of the news tonight," the anchor began, "is an event that has received wide publicity—the Dream Teen Model Search, a national contest sponsored by the Top Ten Modeling Agency. In town for the competition are ten finalists from all over the country, as far away as Hawaii."

The camera panned the models seated in the hospitality suite before coming in for a closeup on Cissy, her dark glasses giving her an air of mystery. The newscaster asked a couple of questions about the injury, finishing with the big one: "Do you think the accident will cause you to lose out in the competition?"

"Possibly," Cissy replied smoothly. "But I'm prepared for that."

You could tell the reporter was surprised. "How do you mean . . . prepared?"

Cissy didn't miss a beat. "After the contest, I'll simply go home to Garden City, Illinois, and continue my education. If it isn't God's will that I be one of the three winners, then I wouldn't want to win. Besides, I'm satisfied just to be one of the contestants."

While the news anchor fumbled for a segue to the next story, Elizabeth turned down the volume.

"Cissy's right, of course. I only hope she can keep her positive outlook if that nasty bruise isn't looking better by Friday night."

What a topsy-tuvy world, Natalie thought as she and Scott headed for the elevator that would take them to the forty-eighth floor. *Up one minute, down the next—or the other way around!* Strange how down she'd been just this afternoon, and now she was on her way—with Scott—to the revolving rooftop restaurant for a romantic dinner for two. And there was not another soul in the elevator with them!

Daring to take a peek, she saw that the lobby of the atrium no longer resembled a Christmas card—it looked more like a postage stamp. Feeling her stomach knot, she lifted her gaze to the dome of the glass elevator and tried to forget that she was traveling on the outside of a wall, rising higher than she'd ever been in her life—except for her plane trip over.

"Wonder if they issue parachutes with this flight." She grinned over at Scott, but her lame joke didn't help much. His nearness did, though, even though it was hard to concentrate on the delicious idea that they were alone together for the first time since arriving in New York.

He looked at her and winked. He didn't seem a bit nervous. Didn't even hold on to the metal strip surrounding the inside of the elevator, while she was hanging on for dear life!

She was beginning to think they would keep going through the rooftop when the elevator came to a shuddering stop and Scott motioned her out onto the carpeted foyer. Light from neighboring buildings filtered through the windows, lending an eerie glow, and mingled with the dim lighting recessed into the ceiling.

With a grown-up confidence that thrilled Natalie, Scott walked up to the stand. "Reservations for Lambert."

The hostess in a white blouse and maroon vest smiled woodenly, but she seemed to warm up after Scott approached. Until then, her smile had seemed about as painted on as her magenta lipstick, Natalie thought.

"One moment please." The woman consulted a seating list and motioned to the maitre d'. "Enjoy your dinner," she called after them as she and Scott followed the man from the stationary floor to the revolving section and took their seats at a table for two next to the window.

As soon as the man was out of earshot, Scott leaned forward. "Bet you never thought you'd be getting the grand tour of Manhattan while going around in circles."

Was he kidding? She'd been going around in circles since the day she'd first laid eyes on him! "You're right. I wouldn't bet on it," she warned. "The waiter has to *find* us first."

She loved the way Scott chuckled, sort of deep in his throat, with little laugh lines crinkling at the corners of his eyes. Maybe he had been looking forward to being with her after all. At least he'd thought of her this afternoon—even with all the excitement of the videotaping and being with Antonio Carlo. Or . . .

maybe he was just being nice. He was like that. Always thinking of other people's feelings.

Natalie looked out the window as the outer rim—floor and skirted tables for two or four—slowly revolved, presenting a panoramic view of the upper stories of buildings—tall, stark, and gray against the sky. She was about to lean over to take a look at the streets below when the waiter came with menus and water.

After one glance at the menu, Natalie gulped. So much for Christmas shopping in New York! She studied the menu, unsure of some of the entrées. Scott would probably know. He'd been practically everywhere, while most of her dining experience consisted of fast food and basic stuff like meat loaf and chicken. "What are you having, Scott?"

"Well, since tomorrow's Thanksgiving, we'll probably be eating turkey. So . . . let's see. The veal medallions with scalloped potatoes looks good to me."

"Me too." With visions of a cow wearing gold medals and potatoes cut with her mom's pinking shears, she folded the menu and laid it aside. She really didn't care what she ate. Being with Scott was enough to whet a girl's appetite, and when the waiter came, she let Scott place their order.

As if on cue, the waiter hurried off just as the restaurant lights dimmed. The night sky deepened to a violet blue, and one after another, stars twinkled on, like diamonds against velvet. She leaned toward the window to see the Christmas lights far below. Every storefront was aglow. Vehicles, like children's toys, crawled along the streets.

"Look," Scott said, his eyes now on the inner circle of the restaurant.

At a table across from them, on the stationary floor, a waiter was peeling an orange. He hoisted the swirled orange peel on the tip of a sharp-pointed knife, struck a match, and flames engulfed the peeling. To one side, just arriving at the door, Natalie thought she glimpsed the three models she'd met this morning—the striking dark-haired girl, and—was it Kameko?—along with their chaperone, she figured. And then they were gone—whisked from view as the restaurant continued on its orbit around the building.

The conversation naturally turned to Cissy and her dilemma.

"I was thinking about what Aunt Liz said—about Cissy's eye," Scott began on a serious note. "We all know how excited she's been about this competition ever since she learned she was one of the finalists." He shrugged. "It can be pretty tough when you want things to go one way . . . and they go another."

He didn't need to tell *her*. She kept hoping Scott would think of her as more than a friend to lean on in the rough times. But so far, she had no real evidence that he cared for her the way she was beginning to care for him. Funny how she'd often tossed off such glib remarks as, "If a guy doesn't like you, you're better off without him." But that was before she met Scott.

"Well," she began, forcing her attention back to the subject, "you know how bold Cissy's been about her faith lately. She'd already given up the idea of a modeling career before she found out about this competition. So if she doesn't win"—Natalie spread her hands—"she'll just trust God to show her what to do next."

Natalie blinked, realizing what she had just said and wondering if she had that much faith where her relationship with Scott was concerned. What if they ended up as nothing more than good friends—ever?

He picked up a packet of sugar and tossed it from one hand to the other. "I guess you're right. But there was a time when I thought I'd turned over all *my* problems to God. You know . . . Mom's alcoholism. Zac seemed pretty together, too. But you know how *that* turned out. I had trouble forgiving Mom, and Zac went on that drinking binge."

Natalie felt such compassion for him. "That must have been terrible for you, Scott. But a lot of good came out of it. You and your mom are closer, and Zac has apparently learned his lesson, too."

Scott reached across the table and laid his hand over hers. "You're really something, you know that, Nat?"

A whole flight of butterflies was doing loops in her stomach. "Really?" She blushed and looked down so he couldn't see her heart in her eyes.

"Yeah. You've meant a lot to our whole family."

Oh, wow. "Thanks." She moved her hand and picked up her water glass to take a sip. He'd just paid her the highest compliment. So why wasn't she thrilled? Katlyn and even Cissy—before they'd become friends—had called her "Miss Goody-Goody." Maybe Scott felt the same way.

"Look at that sky!" he said, breaking the awkward silence between them. "Looks like the angels have decorated for Christmas."

Natalie smiled. She couldn't stay mad at him for

long. "That sounds like something my little sister Rose would say. She's the creative one, you know—like you." Scott was an artist, too, Natalie thought. An artist with a camera instead of a brush. It was his photographs of Cissy that had gotten her this far. Even Antonio recognized his talent.

It sure looked more and more as if Scott was heading toward a very bright future—solo.

He glanced at his watch. "Hey, it's almost eight. You want dessert?"

She shook her head. "I couldn't hold another bite. But here—" she fished for her money in her purse and held it out to him—"I want to pay my part."

He caught her hand. "No way. I *invited* you. *I* pay."

The next thing she knew, he was holding her hand. Just like in the movies. And some of those "angel decorations" were shining in his eyes. She couldn't look away. Then the waiter was interrupting with some dumb question like, "Will there be anything else?"

As they rode the elevator to the thirty-seventh floor, Natalie's heart was still in the clouds. But it wasn't the height or the revolving restaurant that made her head spin. It was the glow of Scott's smile and the look in his eyes that took her breath away.

But was it only friendship he felt . . . or love?

Six

"Pumpkin pie, parades, and pigging out!" announced the TV hostess early Thanksgiving morning. "Welcome to the annual Macy's Thanksgiving Day Parade!"

Although the models had long since left to take their places on the float, Natalie still felt like a fifth wheel. She, along with the two moms and other families of the contest finalists, made her way inside the agency where they had been invited to watch the parade from the windows on the sixth floor of the Herald Square office building.

But she felt much better when Scott invited her along to snap some pictures of the parade from the sidewalk. With the temperature outside hovering just above the freezing mark, they grabbed their hooded parkas and gloves and took off.

Outside, the sidewalks were already jammed with excited onlookers in a holiday mood. Scott took Natalie's arm and steered her to a spot where they could see over the heads of several small children.

"I thought I'd been in crowds before—you know, football games and Christian concerts," she began, glancing up at Scott, "but I've never seen so many people all in one place."

He nodded, scanning the faces. "Something like two million are expected to be out today watching this parade."

"Wow! Wonder if that includes all those people hanging out of the windows." Natalie pointed to the tall buildings, where heads could be seen at almost every opening.

Hearing instruments tuning up and a few shouted instructions, Natalie could tell that the parade was about to begin. The event was kicked off by a band of several hundred young people playing "Celebrate," and she was caught up in the excitement whirling about her. As the floats—elaborate mini-stages—rolled by, Natalie and Scott watched scenes from Broadway plays—*Beauty and the Beast* and *Hello, Dolly*—and Natalie recognized several celebrities. Then there was the Harlem Boys' Choir, singing about brotherhood and love.

When a high school band marched by, led by a line of high-stepping majorettes and cheerleaders waving pompons, Natalie felt a twinge of homesickness. Amy would love this!

"Hi, Amy!" she mouthed, seeing a camera crew working the crowd, then nudged Scott. "I'll bet everyone back home is watching, so I'm going to shout a different name every few seconds."

"Hey, great idea!" Scott laughed and cupped one hand around his mouth. "Hi, Dad! Hi, Zac! Hi, Aunt Martha!"

If he called out Katlyn's name, Natalie didn't hear

it. Anyway, she didn't want to know.

The next action was the Radio City Rockettes, dancing to the tune of "White Christmas." The dancers wore white shorts and swallow-tailed coats, with the tails and long fitted sleeves trimmed in white fur to match the fur around their hats. Natalie was amazed that every step, especially the high kicks, were cookie-cutter perfect. No wonder the Rockettes were world-famous! And that choir behind them wasn't bad, either. "And may all your Christmases be white," they finished as the dancers waved to the crowd and rolled by.

"Snow for Christmas. Wouldn't that be great?" Natalie murmured.

Scott looked down at her and smiled, then pulled her closer with his free hand. "I'll order it for you. Your Christmas present."

Scott was so handsome, even with his nose and cheeks pink from the cold. And if hers were pink, too, then he wouldn't notice that she was blushing to beat the band. Their warm breath mingled in the frosty air, making little puffs of steam above their heads. Natalie's gaze swung back to the scene in front of them, but her heart was turning cartwheels. Christmas present? People didn't exchange presents at Christmas unless they really liked each other. . . .

"Take a look at that guy!" Scott interrupted her daydream. Floating down the street was a bright green-and-orange Dudley the Dragon, the size of a six-story building, and behind him the Top Ten float.

Scott released her to focus his camera for a few still shots.

It was incredible! The front section was one humongous pink rose with green leaves on a bed of white—made entirely of flowers. At the back, about ten feet high, was the numeral 10—also of white flowers—flanked by the Top Ten models in long dresses and fake fur jackets. They were all smiling like models for toothpaste ads. But Cissy, in her tinted designer glasses and standing inside the O, definitely looked like she had the lead.

Spotting Scott and Natalie, she waved and called to them.

The Top Ten float was followed by a clown holding a huge bouquet of balloons in one giant fist. When he began running from one side of the street to the other, handing out balloons, the kids in the crowd went wild. And when Santa Claus appeared on a moving sleigh with his eight reindeer and threw candy into the air and onto the sidewalks, bedlam broke loose.

From behind, someone pushed frantically. Natalie stumbled against Scott, who caught her before she fell. Looking down, she saw a small figure on all fours, scrambling for the treats.

In the confusion a stocking cap came off, and Natalie was stunned to see a tiny gray-haired old woman, wearing a frayed coat and scuffed tennis shoes, clutching an armload of candy and glaring furiously.

"Oh, I'm so sorry! Are you hurt?" Natalie tried to help her to her feet, but the woman held her off with a stern look.

"Stay away from me! I don't need no help. I just come to collect my supper." She got up, still holding on to her candy, and hobbled off down an alley.

Scott snapped a picture, then lowered his camera while staring at the now-deserted entrance.

A gust of cold air whipped through the concrete canyon. "Scott," Natalie said, pulling her hood down more securely over her head, "did you see the holes in her coat?"

"Yeah . . ." he breathed, seemingly unaware of the jostling crowd now breaking up and pushing their way through to their next destination. "She must be freezing."

"Do you think she could be one of those homeless people we read about?"

"Sure looks like it to me."

"How awful, Scott. But . . . what can we do?"

"I don't know, but now that we've seen her, we can't just ignore her, can we?"

Natalie shook her head and followed him toward the entrance to the alley, half expecting to see some thug jump out at them from the dark shadows. But a little way from the corner of the building, they found only the old woman, perched on an orange crate next to a large cardboard box, unwrapping a piece of candy. Nearby, piles of filth and trash littered the alleyway.

"Hello," Scott called softly as they approached. "Don't be afraid. We won't hurt you."

The woman looked up, clasped the candy tightly, and hugged the coat closer to her body. "Get away!" She swatted at him. "Leave me alone!"

"We don't mean you any harm, ma'am," Scott said quickly, stepping back and bumping into Natalie, who was right behind him. "We just wanted to see if there was anything we could do for you."

Her laugh was shrill. "Yeah, call that old geezer in the red suit. Tell 'im he can bring my presents any time now." She chuckled and gathered the tattered coat around her.

"Could we call someone for you . . . help you get home?" Natalie spoke up.

"I *am* home." The woman patted the big cardboard box next to her. "And never mind the man in the red suit. He ain't never give me nothin' yet." The old woman, looking tired and defeated, picked up a tin cup and with shaky fingers, held it out. "Spare a quarter?" she begged, her sad eyes dull and lifeless. "I could use a cuppa coffee."

Natalie felt suddenly drained. She hadn't brought any money with her. She'd been warned that it wasn't safe to be on the streets of New York with a purse.

Scott reached for his belt, unzipped a tiny compartment, and drew out some bills. "Maybe this will help a little." He handed the bills to Natalie.

"All of it?" she whispered.

"Yeah. All of it." He stepped back to take a picture just as Natalie dropped the bills into the tin cup.

The old woman didn't seem to notice the flash but gave them a gap-toothed grin. "Bless ya. You're good kids. Maybe there really *is* a Santy Claus, after all."

All afternoon, even while she was touring the modeling agency with Scott and Antonio, Natalie couldn't get the homeless woman off her mind. She'd read about these people, of course, but she'd never seen one before—at least, not up close. In Garden City, there was that woman who walked the streets a lot. Someone called her a "bag lady" because she carried all her worldly possessions in a shopping bag. But that was all.

As Natalie followed Antonio and Scott through the offices of the agency, then moved into a huge room, her mind was churning. Macy's Thanksgiving Day Parade had officially launched the Christmas season for millions of viewers all over the country. But the razzle-dazzle of the parade and the big city all dressed up in its holiday finery only masked the dirt and grime. And those perfect models, floating on a bed of flowers, painted a picture that was anything but reality. The truth was that there were probably thousands of people in New York just like the little old woman they'd seen today, crawling on her hands and knees to scoop up something to eat off the ground . . . wearing threadbare clothes . . . actually *living* in a cardboard box! She could be somebody's grandmother!

Natalie felt just awful. Up until now, *her* biggest worry had been not where her next meal was coming from, but whether Scott liked her better than Katlyn Chander!

She shook off the worrisome thoughts and moved over to the stage at one side of the room, where Scott was helping Antonio arrange silk trees and large baskets of flowers. From the stage, a long runway jutted out into the room. Rows of chairs had already been set up to accommodate the audience, and camera equipment was strewn about.

"Can I help?" she asked.

Antonio straightened to his full height and stretched, massaging his back. "Sure. You can set those ivy plants in the long boxes along the runway."

"What happened?" she asked him. "You been demoted to janitor?"

Antonio groaned, still rubbing his lower back, and Natalie wondered if he'd hurt himself the night of his little run-in with Cissy. "Don't remind me. I'll hear *that* verdict after the competition." He stooped to lift another ficus tree, and Scott moved over to lend a hand. "In answer to your question, I do a little of everything around here." He slanted Scott a grin. "It's part of the training for a professional photographer."

Natalie got busy with the ivy, wondering if that was how other people managed to "forget" the less fortunate. Just stayed too busy to think of them. She tried again. "I thought the competition was going to be held in the ballroom of the Marriott. So what's going on here?"

"This is where the finalists will practice walking— to be ready for tomorrow night."

"Hey, I learned to walk before I was a year old," Scott quipped.

Antonio shot him a sly look. "Not the way we teach our models to walk."

To Natalie's surprise, Antonio left Scott to finish placing the tree and walked over to kneel beside her on the runway. He was probably going to lecture her on the correct way to arrange ivy.

But he had something else on his mind. "Scott said you guys ran into one of our homeless people today. Said it kind of shook you up."

Natalie nodded. In a way she didn't want to think about it. But at the same time, she was glad Scott hadn't been able to forget the incident either. At least they weren't numb to such things yet.

"There's a lot of that around here, Natalie. But most of the homeless choose to live on the streets. Some of them get more money from welfare or pan-handling than working for a living. And most of them," he said emphatically, "are drunks. She'll probably use your money to buy booze."

Natalie glanced at Scott. If he'd overheard Antonio, what must he be thinking? That the woman could have been his mom? Except, in polite terms, Helen Lambert was an alcoholic . . . not a drunk.

But what was the difference? The only difference Natalie could see was in the way people viewed alco-holism. Scott's mother had a loving, supportive family, a beautiful home, AA meetings, treatment in a sani-tarium if she needed or wanted it, and now, a strong faith in God to carry her through rehabilitation.

But what did this homeless woman have? Just a cardboard box and a tin cup.

She was still mulling it all over when Scott, waiting until Antonio was out of earshot, told her that the models would be having dinner with the Carlos at a trendy restaurant, with a Broadway show afterward. "Since his folks are going to be tied up, mind if I ask Antonio to have Thanksgiving dinner at the hotel with us?"

Natalie shrugged. "Why should I mind?"

But she did. She'd hoped for another romantic eve-ning with Scott—just the two of them.

Still, Thanksgiving was for family. And just like home, at the dinner table, there was always room for one more.

It was during dinner, right after they were served actually, that it happened. Helen asked Scott to say grace. Then everyone dug in, pausing between bites to talk about the parade, how fantastic Cissy looked in her gown and glasses, her chances of winning.

The dressing was delicious, with a yummy white sauce. But one bite was enough to let Natalie know she was going to have a hard time choking down her dinner. Scott, too, was pushing his food around on his plate.

"Something wrong, son?" His mother looked concerned, a little frown rippling across her smooth forehead.

"Yes, Mom, there is," he admitted and pushed away from the table. "There's something I gotta do."

"Are you ill?" Elizabeth Stiles, looking like a slightly older version of Cissy, glanced up from her plate.

He shook his head. "Be back soon. Sorry . . . but I gotta go."

Everybody stared after him as he almost ran out of a rear door of the restaurant. Natalie was pretty sure she knew where he was going. She hoped she did. She picked up her fork. This time the bites went down with no trouble.

Soon, soon now, she thought. She kept watching the door at the rear of the room where she and Scott, Antonio, and the two moms were seated at a table for six. A fancy screen separated them from other diners and gave them the sense of being in their dining room at home. Except that Mom never used a linen tablecloth or her good dishes, if she could help it. With her college classes, homework, and taking care of their family, it was all she could do to serve on the kitchen table with paper napkins and the everyday dishes.

It was about time Scott was getting back. If she was right, he'd only had a couple of blocks to walk—and back. Yes! There he was now . . . and he had the little homeless woman with him—stocking cap, shabby coat, and all!

Scott led her to the table, her arm through his—just like she was Queen Elizabeth or something. "This is my new friend, Gertrude. You've met Natalie, of course." He introduced everyone else, and Gertrude smiled weakly. "Could I take your coat?"

"No! It's mine!" she said quickly and jerked her arm away, holding the front of her buttonless coat with both grimy hands. "They give it to me at the Goodwill!"

It would have been hilarious, Natalie thought, except that it was so pathetic.

"Sure, Gertrude. Sure." Scott backed away, both hands up before him, then tried to get her settled at the table between himself and Natalie. He widened his eyes and shrugged.

Natalie leaned over to explain. "Don't worry, Gertrude. No one here wants to take anything that belongs to you. The waitress will bring your dinner. Oh, there she is, Scott."

He placed the order while his mother and aunt composed themselves after one initial gasp. Natalie could understand how they must be feeling. Antonio only grinned and shook his head as if he was not believing this.

Elizabeth Stiles graciously took up the conversation just like she was having dinner with the mayor's wife or one of the ladies in her bridge club. "And how did you and my nephew meet . . . Gertrude?"

Before the woman could answer, the waitress had placed a turkey dinner in front of her, and Gertrude started shoveling in the food.

Scott grinned. "Let's just say that Nat and I . . . uh . . . ran into her, Mom, at the parade this morning."

Natalie stifled a giggle. *Or the other way around!*

Determined to make conversation, Helen Lambert tried again. "Do you live around here?"

"Right up the street," Gertrude said without looking up or missing a bite.

Behind his hand, Antonio mouthed, "In the alley." Two pairs of well-groomed eyebrows lifted.

Elizabeth cleared her throat, a look of bewilderment still on her face. "My, what a delicious dinner."

"Yep. I like *this* stuff the best," Gertrude said with her mouth full, stabbing the dressing with her fork.

"That's my favorite, too." Natalie looked over at Scott, who was wolfing down his own meal. He hadn't looked this happy since arriving in the Big Apple.

"You saw the parade, then, Gertrude?" Helen asked.

"Seen 'em all."

It seemed a safe enough topic, so everyone joined in, rehashing the day for the second time while Gertrude finished her pumpkin pie. Finally, with a huge sigh, she wiped her mouth with the back of her sleeve and sat back, looking around her for the first time. "They cook pretty good in here."

"Hey, Scott," Antonio leaned forward to whisper, "why don't you take a shot of everyone at the table . . . as a keepsake."

Gertrude's faded gray eyes grew wide with horror. "Shot?"

Natalie had to smile. Of course! Why wouldn't the woman think of guns? And with Antonio—with his dark good looks and his pin-striped jacket—looking like a young member of the Mafia. . . . "Oh, that's just a term photographers use, Gertrude," she assured the frightened old lady. "Antonio just meant he wanted Scott to take a picture with his camera."

Scott held up the camera that he'd parked under his chair during dinner.

Gertrude waved her hand in the air. "Don't want no pictures of me," she said. "But I would like one of this boy . . . to remember him by"—turning to Natalie, she added—"and this little sweetheart here."

But the woman consented to having her picture taken after Scott persuaded the waitress to snap several of all of them.

Natalie wondered what the other people in the restaurant would think if they could see the little group behind the screen. Elizabeth and Helen—elegant society women, with their shiny blond hair beautifully styled and their designer after-five suits. Scott and Antonio, who looked like models themselves in their jackets and ties. Natalie had dressed for dinner, too, in the burgundy velvet she'd brought for a special occasion.

And then there was Gertrude—with her thin, graying hair standing out in wisps where she'd pulled off her cap, and her pitiful, threadbare coat with no buttons. What the eye of the camera couldn't see was her scuffed tennis shoes under the table. From rags to riches—all at this one table!

For a few minutes on this Thanksgiving Day, Natalie had been a little homesick for her family. But sitting here—beside Gertrude—gave *thanksgiving* a whole new definition. And family, she decided, was much more than the folks who lived under your roof.

Glancing across at Scott, her heart swelled. The look he gave her would have melted a snowman in January. If she had only this one memory of him—it was enough . . . almost.

Seven

Cissy was one big nerve!

She'd never had the jitters like this before. Not even when she'd modeled in fashion shows, served as president of the student council in high school, made speeches at college, or given her personal testimony in churches about her experience during the tornado last spring.

But a little normal apprehension was nothing like this paralyzing fear that left her feeling too weak to walk. Her hand even trembled when she applied the concealer over the sickly greenish-purple quarter-moon beneath her eye.

For three days, she'd been telling herself it didn't matter if she wasn't chosen as one of the top three contestants to be put under contract by the modeling agency and receive a college scholarship. Unlike some of these girls, she didn't really need the money. And she'd told everyone—including a national TV viewing audience—that she was "prepared" to lose. It wasn't that she was putting up a big front. She'd developed some real friends among the other nine girls as they'd spent time together being briefed, photographed, and interviewed by TV and newspaper reporters. And there had been some down time, during dinners with the Carlos or Big Mac snacks, when they could get to know each other. They'd received plenty of instruction, too, on how to walk, stand, sit, and smile. Too bad there were no lessons on how to *feel*.

Something had changed during dinner tonight. Now, instead of exchanging information about each other or cracking jokes, there was a tension that was winding tighter by the minute. The competition was the only topic of conversation. It didn't help any when Tomas Carlo reminded them that among the guests would be scouts on the lookout for various kinds of models—runway, magazine ad models, even models for television commercials, which would require a certain amount of acting ability. If nothing else, some of the girls would be offered a one-time modeling assignment.

So everyone was hoping for something big. And everyone was uptight. Ardath spilled coffee all over her new blouse and snapped at the waitress, who took longer than she should have to bring a towel. Heather dropped her fork in her lap. It bounced once and clattered onto the floor. "I'd cry if it wouldn't ruin my makeup!" she wailed.

That broke the ice a little, and they laughed, relieved to focus on something besides their own fears.

Cissy choked on her first bite and gave up. If the competition didn't end soon, she'd be a candidate for a psychiatrist's office! Then, touching the little dove dangling at the end of a silver chain around her neck, she was ashamed of herself. *I'm not alone*, she remembered. *God is with me—win or lose. But I do wish I could see Him right now!* Selena's knowing wink across the table was like an answer to her prayer. Cissy had shared her story with the younger girl, and they'd prayed together every night. She took a deep breath.

Back in the room, as they all prepared for the big event at eight o'clock, she and Selena listened to the others in the adjoining room muttering and complaining. "Oh no! I smeared my lipstick!" or "Of all times to have a bad hair day!"

At least Cissy didn't have that worry. She was grateful that the cut of her own baby-fine hair allowed it to fall right in place with only a little blow-drying. She had also learned to shampoo several hours before an event. She'd done hers that afternoon, while many of the girls had waited until evening.

But they had one advantage she didn't have, Cissy was thinking. *No one else has a black eye!* She had dabbed on tons of concealer, and now the area under her eye felt as if it were loaded with cement and would dry, crack, and fall off—right in the middle of the competition. Oh well, if she lost, at least she had a good reason.

She thought of Selena's three reasons why she *could* win. One, she was a Christian, and both of them knew that prayer changes things. Two, the Carlos might think she would sue if she didn't win, since her mishap had been caused by their own son. And three, Antonio Carlo liked her—or so Selena said. That couldn't hurt a thing, since his opinion would carry a lot of weight with his parents and the contest officials.

Antonio liked her? How did Selena get that?

About the time Cissy was beginning to enjoy the idea, she remembered Selena's second comment. Maybe

Antonio was only being nice to avoid a suit! Cissy reviewed her last conversation with her mom. They had been allowed only telephone contact since Wednesday, but her mother had mentioned how well Scott and "the Carlo boy" were getting along. "Seems they've struck up quite a friendship." She had laughed then. "I suppose it's their common interest in photography."

But Cissy wasn't so sure. Maybe there was something to Selena's speculation. Still, she was only fourteen. She probably just blurted out whatever came to mind. . . .

But when Selena was ready for the competition and twirled in front of Cissy for her approval, she looked like anything but a fourteen-year-old! She was a knockout with that mass of auburn curls tumbling down her back and framing her pretty face. And her huge green eyes caught the sparkle of her sequined dress that complemented her trim figure.

Looks wasn't the only thing Selena Raintree had going for her, Cissy thought. There was an inner glow that didn't come from bottles or jars or all the makeup tips in the world!

Cissy had chosen a simple but elegant style for herself, knowing that her blond looks were best displayed against a dramatic background. Her stark black gown, with its tiny straps that crossed in back, was not as glittery as Selena's, but it, too, was made of a fabric that reflected the light and gleamed like the diamond necklace and earrings she was wearing.

"You look terrific, Cissy!" Selena was all smiles. "There's still just a tad of that bruise under your eye. But maybe the judges will think it's some new makeup technique. Come on. Let's go wow 'em!"

Cissy shrugged and followed Selena from the room. *This is the best I can do, Lord,* she prayed. *The rest is up to you.*

———

When it was time to dress for the evening, Natalie wasn't sure what to wear. Her new long A-line white skirt and angora sweater? The velvet skirt and ivory blouse? Or . . . her prom dress? She'd brought it in case they went formal. Still unable to make up her mind, she laid all the outfits on the bed and called in the two women to ask their opinion.

Elizabeth Stiles was the first to speak up. "Oh, they're all so pretty, Natalie. You have such lovely taste."

That's because your daughter helped me! Natalie thought but kept that little secret to herself.

"This is a glamorous occasion," Helen reminded them. "And if Cissy wins, we're all going to be in the limelight. So let's give them something to look at! I'd say the black and white."

"You're right," Helen agreed, running a finger over the taffeta skirt. "This is the very thing."

It was the dress Natalie had worn to the Junior Prom last year—the prom that Scott had *not* taken her to, although she'd expected him to ask her. So she'd ended up going with Stick Gordon rather than staying home or going alone.

What a disappointment! But looking back on that fiasco, she had to smile. It seemed a lifetime ago. She had imagined wearing this dress somewhere special with Scott. But never in a million years would she have imagined she'd be in New York with him, on her way to a nationally televised model contest!

Excitement tingled through her as she dressed, then gave herself the once-over in the mirror. Wow! Was this the same Natalie Ainsworth—plain vanilla, no-frills Natalie?

The off-the-shoulder bodice, with its spaghetti straps, lay smoothly against her skin. She'd filled out a little since the prom, but it was kind of flattering, she admitted to herself. The top tapered to a full black-and-white checked skirt that fell just above her knees. Sheer black hose and heels with rhinestone clips were the perfect accessories, along with her mom's small rhinestone earrings. And although she preferred the natural look, for tonight she'd applied a light touch of makeup the way Cissy had taught her. "Not too shabby, girl," she told her reflection in the mirror.

"Stunning!" chorused the two women when she emerged into the sitting room.

"Thanks. And you both look wonderful." But that was nothing new. The women were so stylish and had terrific figures. Natalie suspected they worked at it—like her mom did in the mornings. Helen looked so pretty in a deep red silk dress that fell elegantly to midcalf, her ruby and diamond jewelry setting it off to perfection. And Natalie could tell where Cissy got her good looks. Elizabeth Stiles could have been Cissy's older sister in her light blue dress that shimmered when she moved with a silvery glow. Her jewelry was sapphires and diamonds—the real thing, Natalie was sure.

Feeling like an ornament on a Christmas tree, Natalie rode with Helen and Elizabeth to the eighth floor, then took the escalator to the fifth-floor ballroom. At the door, they were told where to find their name tags that would indicate their table number.

Elizabeth led the way to table thirty, which turned out to be a great location—six rows from the stage and right beside the runway, flanked with pots of ivy set in deep containers. Natalie could easily see that this was an enlarged version of the agency's practice room.

Cissy's mom was thrilled with their seating. "We'll be able to see her up close from here."

Natalie hadn't been able to figure out how the event could be staged on two floors—the fifth and sixth—until she took her seat and looked around. The fifth floor was a huge cavern of a room, with the sixth forming a balcony around the sides and back, where spectators— the rest of the studio audience, she learned—could look down on the stage. A huge crystal chandelier, with prisms like giant icicles, hung suspended from the ceiling of the upper floor, with smaller versions beneath the balcony.

So this is the world of glamour, Natalie thought, *but where's Scott?* Just at that moment, he appeared, along with Antonio, who let out a long wolf whistle when he spotted Natalie.

"Are you sure you shouldn't be *on* that runway instead of sitting *beside* it?" His gaze swept her from the top of her head to the rhinestone clips on her high heels. "As an employee of the Top Ten Modeling Agency, I'd give you a ten!"

Scott's big grin told her he thought so, too. "How about a shot of Nat and me?" He handed Antonio his camera. "Right here, with the flowers on the table in the foreground."

Natalie thought she'd pass out when Scott moved over to put his arm around her waist. He wanted a picture of just the two of them!

Antonio snapped the picture with Scott laughing down at her. And *she*? Well, she was absolutely positive her feelings for him were written all over her face.

"One more." Antonio took aim and snapped the shutter the second time, then gave them a thumbs-up. "You two look . . ."

But whatever he was about to say was interrupted when another couple—the parents of a model, Kathleen Carson—joined them at their table, leaving two seats free, one of which Antonio promptly took. While the adults got acquainted, Scott and Antonio filled Natalie in on the afternoon's events.

"Gertrude agreed to let Antonio take some pictures," Scott began. "She'll stay at the shelter over the weekend, and they'll start looking for some help for her on Monday morning. The poor old girl came here on a bus from New Jersey, where she was evicted from her apartment after her son died. Thought she'd have a better chance of making it on the streets of a big city."

"How sad." Natalie was genuinely sorry for the old woman and looked at Scott with new appreciation. He wasn't just talking about the problem—he was doing something. "I'm really glad you're helping her."

He gave a wry grin. "I don't think I'd have followed her into that alley if you hadn't been with me, Nat," he admitted. "By the way, Gertrude asked about you. Said you're a beautiful girl . . . and I shouldn't let you get away."

Natalie laughed nervously and fiddled with the

stem of her water goblet. "Must have been a case of mistaken identity."

Scott leaned closer and looked right into her eyes. "There's no mistake, Nat. Gertie may be missing a cog or two, but she knows a good-looking girl when she sees one. And *I'm* looking at the most beautiful girl in the room."

Natalie felt her cheeks burn, but in the next second, the flame went out like it had been doused with a blast of ice water. "At the moment I'm the *only* girl in the room under twenty-one," she reminded him. "Just wait until the models come on."

"Not one of them will be prettier than you—in that great dress you're wearing."

"Oh, *this* old thing?" She couldn't resist rubbing it in a little. "This was my prom dress—the prom you managed to avoid."

"Ouch! So *that's* what I missed?" Scott's grin faded. He looked truly repentant, and Natalie knew he was thinking of the night he'd left town with his dad to visit his mother in the alcoholic rehabilitation center. He hadn't even known that his cousin had told Natalie he planned to ask her to the prom, or that she'd waited and wondered until the last minute. "You know how sorry I am . . . about . . . everything."

Natalie was sorry, too—that she'd brought it up.

Just then dinner was served, and everyone turned their attention to the yummy-looking food in front of them. The dishes were probably five-star—like everything else around here—but she couldn't taste very much of it. Even when the dessert was presented with a flourish—chocolate mousse cake iced in a red rose with green leaves and topped with a little white flag imprinted with the letters spelling out TOP TEN—she only picked at it.

When the dessert plates were removed and water glasses refilled, Antonio excused himself. "I've got to go down front now. See you guys later." He hurried off.

Elizabeth glanced at her watch. "It's almost eight o'clock."

"Places, everyone!" boomed a male voice as narrow beams of colored light swept the stage. Someone began a countdown, and Natalie felt the electricity charging the room as the announcer began, "Welcome to the ninth annual Top Ten Dream Teen Model Search, held in New York City—city of ten million dreams!"

As a chorus in the background belted out a rousing rendition of "New York, New York," the Carlos were illuminated by a single spotlight. Maria, wearing a gold, floor-length sheath, looked like she'd been touched by King Midas. And her handsome husband was the perfect companion in a black tux with golden lapels and cummerbund. The smiling couple bowed and walked over to a side lectern where they took turns giving a brief history of the agency and introduced the judges.

Then Tomas took center stage. "Every finalist you see here tonight is a winner in her own right. The ultimate decision will be based on poise, beauty, and photogenic quality. As our studio audience knows, the top three models chosen tonight will each be awarded a contract with our agency and a substantial scholarship to the school of her choice. Let the judging begin!"

Cued by another lively tune by the orchestra, playing in a pit under the stage, the parade of gorgeous girls began. The audience began to rise, table by table—even in the balcony—until everyone was standing and applauding. The applause continued as each girl took her turn coming to center stage, while the photo from which she was chosen was shown on a huge screen behind her.

Natalie had seen Cissy's portfolio, and what followed was like a portfolio come to life. Each finalist was shown on the screen above the stage, while the Carlos conversed with her briefly, asking questions about her background, her school and family, and her career plans.

Since the girls were interviewed alphabetically, Cissy was the seventh to be questioned. From a distance her bad eye wasn't noticeable. But on the big screen, her heavy makeup was pretty obvious, along with the one brow that was not perfectly arched. Maria mentioned the injury, saying only that it had been an accident, that no permanent damage had been done, and that in the tradition of a true professional, Cissy was going on with the show.

Natalie wondered if that explanation was intended for the benefit of anyone who might question why Cissy—with her one tiny flaw—was in the competition at all. But even with the injured eye, she was beautiful to Natalie. And the best part was that her beauty was more than skin deep!

When asked about her future plans, Cissy spoke right up. "I don't know what my future holds, but I know Who holds my future."

"Can you believe she said that?" Scott whispered to Natalie. "She's the greatest!" After her brief interview, Cissy again paraded across the stage, then exited through a side curtain.

When Antonio's videotape of the models in the hospitality suite on Thursday morning was shown, Cissy—in her dark glasses—was the most conspicuous.

"And there *you* are, Nat," Scott pointed out. Sure enough, in the background were Natalie and Beth, laughing and talking as they served juice and coffee across the counter. *Well*, Natalie thought, *I don't look too dumb*. As a matter of fact, she appeared to fit in quite well—at least on the sidelines.

In some other footage was a shot of Scott, surrounded by several of the girls and looking pretty happy about the whole thing. Natalie couldn't help feeling a tiny stab of jealousy.

Instead of a swimsuit segment, each of the girls appeared in casual attire, acting out a favorite sport or hobby. Selena came out in tennis gear, complete with sweatbands and racket, her mass of red hair pulled back with a ribbon. With a tennis court setting on the big screen behind her, she took a few practice swings, showing a winning form.

Ardath was in a basketball uniform, holding a ball under one arm. She dribbled the ball a couple of times, balanced and spun it in one palm, then finished with a jump shot.

Heather looked like a snow bunny in a pink ski suit trimmed in fur. Somehow they had rigged up a pair of cross country skis on a track, and she faked the moves, making it appear that she was skimming the stage, a winter snowscape rolling past on the screen behind.

When the scene changed again, the snow had melted into summer, and a tropical beach replaced the rolling hills. This time it was Cissy, wearing a modest one-piece swimsuit with coverup and a straw hat that dipped over one eye. *Good camouflage job, Cissy!* Natalie applauded her silently.

Since there was no way to demonstrate her swimming skills, Cissy took the microphone and spoke, instead, about safety in the sun—using the right sunscreen, avoiding the peak hours. And then, to Natalie's surprise, she wound up with a completely unexpected comment: "God has created a beautiful world—sun and stars, oceans and mountains, plains and valleys. And He created *us*. We all look different on the outside—different facial features, different hair color, different body build." She gestured toward the sunny beach pictured behind her. "Like grains of sand, none of us are alike. But we can all be beautiful on the inside. No matter who comes out on top tonight, we can all be better people because we've learned to work together and to love each other—regardless of our differences. Thank you."

Cissy left the stage to a deafening roar of applause, followed by the next three finalists, who completed the second round of the judging.

Then, after station identification, the third phase of the contest—the costume division—began. Again the girls walked onstage and down the runway, some in the costumes of their native origin; others, as storybook characters. The big screen spotlighted the individual finalists, while Maria Carlo narrated their choice of costume. Kameko was dressed in a Japanese kimono with butterfly sleeves while the orchestra played "South Pacific." Ardath appeared in a brightly patterned wrap dress with matching turban. And Kathleen, in an Irish peasant's dress. Selena, in white shorts and a blue jacket with stars, her red hair streaming behind her, personified the American flag to the tune of "America the Beautiful." Judging by the audience reaction, Natalie figured Selena was strongly in the lead.

But it was Cissy who stole the show. The last contestant to appear, she was wearing a wedding gown, which was "every girl's dream, no matter what her nationality or ethnic background," Maria commented.

You've done it again, Cissy! Used your handicap to your advantage! Natalie was thinking as her friend, her fingertip veil covering all signs of the bruise, paraded to the end of the runway, accompanied by a lush instrumental version of "The Wedding Song." When she turned slowly to walk back, her long cathedral-length train trailing behind, the tempo changed dramatically. This time, the orchestra created a moment of reverence as the chorus joined them for "The Lord's Prayer."

Stepping to center stage, Cissy bowed her head, crowned with flowers. Then, with the last chord lingering in the air, she drifted offstage in a cloud of white, leaving the audience breathless. It was several seconds before they were on their feet, giving her a standing ovation that lasted long past the "cut" signal that brought this segment to an end.

Natalie could hardly see for the tears. But she felt Scott's hand reach for hers and squeeze—hard. Cissy was going to win. She just *knew* it!

Eight

"The envelope, please."

A hush fell over the audience as a judge rose from his seat down front and handed the verdict to Tomas Carlo. Cissy held her breath. Winning wasn't everything. She knew that. So why was her heart permanently lodged in her throat?

It seemed forever before Mr. Carlo managed to tear the envelope open. But he didn't read off the names of the winners right away. Instead, he launched into another long-winded speech. "As we have mentioned before, every Top Ten finalist is already a winner, with the possibility of receiving—in addition to a $500 gift certificate from Macy's—an offer for a short-term modeling assignment.

"But for three lucky young women, tonight will be a dream come true, a doorway to the future. Along with a one-year contract with our agency goes a $10,000 scholarship to the college of her choice."

There was a pause for audience reaction. Cissy grew warm, then cold. She felt like the heroine in an Agatha Christie mystery—the one entitled *Then There Were None*.

They had started the contest with ten finalists, all of whom stood here now, looking poised and radiant—at least on the outside. Inside, Cissy was sure they were all quaking in their high heels—just as she was. They would end the evening with three winners—and seven losers!

Since the winners were to be announced alphabetically, she wasn't too concerned when the first name to be called was "Kathleen Carson." Cissy noticed the distinguished-looking couple at her mom's table hugging each other and applauding wildly.

Then there were nine. Cissy continued to smile brightly, although her cheeks ached with the effort. *Two more to go.*

This time it was Maria Carlo who took the microphone. "Winner number two is . . . Ardath Jackson!"

The tall African-American, flashing her white teeth, stepped up to shake hands with the Carlos and receive her roses. With her usual pizzazz, she held the bouquet high above her head in a gesture of victory. Cissy couldn't begrudge Ardath her win. She'd gotten to know the girl pretty well in the past few days and had learned that she'd come up the hard way and had made something of herself. She deserved this break.

And then there were eight. Eight girls, still waiting for their chance at stardom. They held hands, forming a chain across the stage, glancing nervously at the audience, then at each other. Cissy closed her eyes, hearing the buzz of voices, the background music, the drum roll. *Please, Lord. . . .*

But it was Selena Raintree's name that Tomas Carlo read out. Her roommate! Selena with the sizzling hair and the sweet southern accent. Who wouldn't love her? Cissy clapped louder than anyone as the third winner accepted her bouquet and blew a kiss to the judges.

But Cissy couldn't quite squelch the sting of disappointment when, at the end of the telecast, the media stormed the stage to interview the winners, shoving microphones under their noses and shouting rapid-fire questions.

Then there were seven . . . who retreated to the hospitality suite to lick their wounds. Cissy couldn't believe it! She thought she'd done so well. She'd been able to cover her bruise okay, and the outfits she'd chosen had helped, too. Judging from the audience's reaction, she should have won!

Cissy and the others were just beginning to confess their letdown about the outcome of the evening when the Carlos rushed in with an encouraging word for everyone and exciting news for two others.

"A teen magazine editor is interested in Heather, and a movie scout is ready to discuss a screen test with Courtney," announced a radiant Maria Carlo. "And don't worry. Most of you will be hearing from an agent sometime in the future. Just consider tonight a real publicity opportunity."

It was over. Cissy hadn't won a thing, and now all she wanted was to get back to her room and chalk this up as an experience she didn't care to repeat any time soon. Being a loser was no fun. In fact, this whole thing bordered on becoming a real downer—something she hadn't felt since the night of the tornado.

Just about the time she was gathering up her things to leave, Antonio shot through the door, followed by a man with a camera slung around his neck. The craggy face sported a stubble of beard as if he hadn't taken time to shave, and his hair was tousled. *The Columbo type,* Cissy decided. Even his dark suit and tie seemed out of character. He'd look more natural in a ratty old trench coat.

He scoped out the room, his eagle eyes apparently taking in everything in a sweeping glance. His gaze settled on her for a second before he turned to accept the manila folder Antonio was handing him. Well, whatever it was obviously didn't concern *her.*

Cissy sank down on a couch. She might as well wait for her family to get here. She could leave with them. But the weird feeling of rejection lingered. And when she saw Scott and Natalie heading her way, she jumped to her feet. If anyone tried to console her . . .

She spoke up before they could get a word out. "Now that the competition's over, we can move you into my room, Nat."

Elizabeth, who had been trailing the others, stepped up to give Cissy a hug. "Honey, the Carlos have asked us to stay for a while. They have something to discuss with us."

Cissy took a deep breath. Did she dare get her hopes up again?

"Sorry to keep you so late, folks," Tomas began, coming over to join them. "But I wanted you to meet Jack Henderson of the *Times.* We've done business together for years, and he has a proposition that might interest some of you."

"It's about these photos," the craggy-faced man began, sliding some glossy prints from the manila folder.

Could those be some more pictures Scott made of me? Cissy wondered. Must be, because her cousin was looking more than pleased with himself.

"Hey, those turned out pretty good," Scott was saying as he moved in closer to take a look at the photographs spread out on a coffee table.

"We thought so, too." Maria stepped up to stand beside her husband. "That's why we called Jack. It's just that we haven't had a minute all weekend—with the competition, you understand." She glanced at Cissy. "Cissy here knows better than anyone."

Yeah. She knew, all right.

Thinking she might still have a chance at something, Cissy leaned forward to get a better view of the photos . . . and was shocked at what she saw. These were not shots of her . . . or any of the other models, for that matter. The woman in these pictures had to be at least a hundred and two!

There was one of Natalie and the old woman in an alley, with Nat dropping some money into a tin cup. In another, the woman was with Cissy's family having dinner in the hotel restaurant. And there were several of the woman in a shelter of some sort.

"Not only are these good quality pictures," Jack Henderson was saying. "They're much more than that. There's a first-rate human interest angle here." He turned to Scott. "Antonio tells me you're only seventeen, son."

Scott gulped. "Yes, sir. A senior in high school."

The guy smiled for the first time, fine lines crinkling at the corners of his eyes. "Good copy. 'Young Tourist Helps the Homeless.' " He leaned back, his hands clasped behind his head. "The story's all right here." Resting his elbows on his knees now, he looked Scott in the eye. "I'd like to buy these photos from you, son, and run them in Sunday's paper, along with the story of how you got acquainted with the homeless woman." He named a price.

There was a moment of shocked silence, and Scott glanced over at his mother. "Mom?" he squeaked, sounding more like Stick Gordon, whose voice seemed permanently cracked.

She smiled and shrugged. "They're your pictures, Scott. It's your decision what you do with them."

Scott turned beet red and began to stammer. "I don't . . . I mean, I . . ."

"Come on, pal." Antonio laughed, relieving the awkward moment, then faked a right hook to Scott's jaw. "Cut the modesty act. If you're going to be a professional, you gotta learn how to wheel and deal. Do you know how many seasoned photographers would give their eyeteeth to be in your shoes right now?"

Scott grimaced and murmured, "I think I just swallowed mine."

Amid the good-natured laughter that followed, Jack waited out Scott's answer.

Finally, Scott cleared his throat. "I had help," he admitted. "If it wasn't for Natalie here, I probably wouldn't even be around to care about a homeless woman."

Jack lifted his heavy brows. "If you let me do this story, it'll carry *my* byline . . . although I couldn't write the piece without you."

There was a slight pause while Scott considered the

reporter's words. "I get your point. So . . . okay. What's next?"

Jack got to his feet. "This is where we wrap up the deal." He glanced around the room. "How about over there—out of the way?"

While the two were talking in an alcove of the hospitality suite, Maria approached Cissy. It was the moment she had been dreading.

"Cissy, do you feel that your . . . accident . . . lost you the contest?"

"Maybe," she said honestly. "But I also believe God didn't want me to win."

"Then you think *God* pushed Antonio into you that night and caused you to fall?" Maria seemed horrified.

Cissy saw the good-looking Italian stiffen. She certainly didn't want Antonio to think she blamed *him*. After a moment, she tried to express her thoughts. "I think Antonio just wasn't watching where he was going. But God could have prevented what happened . . . if He'd wanted to. For some reason, He didn't intervene—this time." Maria's puzzled expression encouraged Cissy to go on. "But He *did* turn me around in a tornado once—and saved my life."

Antonio walked nearer and stood behind the big lounge chair where Jack had been sitting. "You mean," he asked, resting his arms on the high back, "you really were caught in a tornado?"

"Yes," she admitted somewhat reluctantly. "When I was young and foolish . . . on my way to elope with my boyfriend."

Antonio's lips twitched a little, making that intriguing little dimple at the corner of his mouth. He seemed really interested.

"I don't suppose you'd care to talk about it," Maria said kindly.

Cissy shrugged and glanced over at her family and Natalie. "I've talked about it all over southern Illinois . . . why not New York?"

"Hold on just a minute." Tomas lifted his hand and called to his friend. "You'd better hear this, Jack. We may have another story here. And I think I've come up with the perfect headline!"

———

Cissy was feeling numb with fatigue after her umpteenth retelling of the tornado story—how she'd been sucked up as if by a vacuum into the eye and was drawn closer to God through a little white bird. At that, they had listened even more attentively as she explained Natalie's youth group's White Dove campaign.

"I'm impressed," Antonio said out in the hallway after they'd all said their good-nights. "I've never met a girl who was more concerned with her faith than her face and figure."

She laughed lightly. "You're in the beauty business. You know that models have to be concerned about all that."

"I suppose." He shrugged. "But you aren't like the others. I noticed that the very first time I met you."

His great smile and twinkling dark eyes hoisted her spirits higher than they had been all evening. It occurred to her that he must have a million women after him—all *winners*. She started to brush past him on her way to her room, but he stopped her with another question.

"Are you still feeling pretty rotten . . . about Ron, I mean?"

She gave a short, surprised laugh. "Not at all."

"But you were going to marry him."

"You missed the point," she explained. "I was eloping with him because I was angry with my parents. Not because I . . ."

She looked up into his questioning eyes, and he finished for her, "Not because you loved him."

"Oh, at one time, I thought I loved him. But if I did, it was the puppy variety."

A chuckle formed deep in Antonio's throat, and that drop-dead smile spread across his handsome face. He leaned forward as if he had something else to say just as Scott and Natalie walked up. Then his mood shifted, and he turned to include them. "How about the four of us going ice skating in the morning?"

"Ice skating?" Cissy was skeptical. "Isn't it too early in the season?"

"Rockefeller Center," he explained. "It's not far from here. I could pick you guys up, see that you're all fitted with skates."

Scott gave an impish frown and poked his cousin in the arm. "Cissy never tries anything dangerous that might interfere with her modeling."

She was about ready to agree with him when she looked into the dark depths of Antonio's eyes—and changed her mind. What difference did it make? She already had one black eye . . . and the competition was over.

"Sounds like fun. Let's go for it!"

Exhausted from the days of tension surrounding

the competition—and the fact that it was almost midnight—Cissy was ready to drop by the time she and Natalie got settled in her room. She'd always tried to get plenty of rest to avoid those puffy little lumps beneath her eyes. Now it didn't matter. Besides, she had more important things on her mind.

"You know, Nat, Selena kept saying she and I would win because we were both Christians. Yet, she wasn't outspoken about her faith, and I was." She clamped her hand over her mouth. "Boy, that must sound like sour grapes."

Natalie hung her last outfit in the closet, then turned to face Cissy. "Not really. Every year my sister Amy gets uptight about going out for cheerleading, and she'd be devastated if she didn't make it. But that doesn't make her less of a Christian. It just means she's human."

Sitting cross-legged on her bed, Cissy picked up a pillow and wrapped her arms around it. "I'm sincerely glad all three girls won—especially Ardath—but I can't help but wonder how God's will for me fits into all this."

Natalie pondered a minute before replying. "Maybe He wanted them to win so He can teach them what you already know." She looked up to see Cissy's mystified expression. "Maybe He wants to teach them that modeling—or anything else, for that matter—is not the answer. Jesus is."

Cissy shook her head. "How did you get so wise so young? I guess I tend to forget God has a purpose for others, too, and focus on myself."

"We *all* do. But I think you're taking this whole thing really well."

"Do I have a choice?" Cissy grinned and spread her

hands. "No, seriously, I think God is teaching me humility. That's something else that seems to come naturally to you, Nat."

Maybe it's because I'm a born loser flashed through Natalie's mind as she closed her now-empty suitcase and shoved it in the back of the closet. *At least Cissy was a finalist in the competition. I wasn't even in the running.*

Cissy didn't seem to notice that she hadn't said a word. "You know, I think I understand Selena's attitude a little. It would be very tempting to keep quiet about my faith and compete with other girls for Antonio's attention. Can't you just see me floating around New York with that gorgeous guy, making everyone else jealous?" She giggled and fell back against the bed.

That wasn't hard to do. The two of them made a great-looking couple. Cissy—so blond and fair. Antonio—tall, dark, and handsome. "I can see it all now."

"Who knows?" Cissy gave a secretive little smile as she hopped up from the bed, grabbed her boxers and top, and went into the bedroom to scrub her face free of makeup and apply night cream. She was back in no time. "Your turn, Nat."

Cissy was in bed when Natalie returned to the room. "Ready for lights out? You must be wiped."

"Yeah. Night, Nat. And thanks . . . for everything."

It took a while for Cissy's eyes to adjust to the near total darkness of the room. Only a flat, dull gloom pressed against the drapes, a faint gray streak visible at one edge where the light seeped in. All sorts of things whirled through her mind. Why? Why? Why was she feeling these unwanted emotions, and *why* hadn't she won?

She took a deep breath, then let it out in a sigh. "You asleep?" she called softly.

"No. Want to talk?"

"You're always there for other people, Natalie, so I think you'll understand this. Deep down, I really do want God's will for my life. You've helped me realize that. But I'll have to admit, I *am* disappointed about tonight. Even embarrassed. I feel . . . like a failure. It really does bother me that God might not want to use me in modeling or acting."

There was a long silence, and Cissy was beginning to feel like the bottom had dropped out of everything when Natalie spoke up. "I don't think He works that way, Cissy. He wouldn't call you into something you don't like or don't have an aptitude for."

"I hope you're right." Cissy paused, then asked a little hesitantly, "Nat, would you pray for me . . . that I'll have the right attitude?"

"Sure." To Cissy's total surprise, Natalie started right in, praying out loud. "And, dear God," Natalie added, "help us not to get upset when you don't do our will, on our timetable, at our convenience. Give us the patience to wait on you. And we praise you for all you have already given us—especially your son, Jesus Christ, who died for our sins. Amen."

"You just taught me something else, Nat," Cissy said after a long pause. "If most people are like I am, they say they'll pray for you . . . but if they do, it's in private. I love the way *you* do it—right on the spot."

Natalie laughed softly into the darkness. "I learned

that the hard way myself—from making promises and then forgetting to follow through."

"You're very special, Natalie Ainsworth, you know that?" Cissy whispered. "Now get some sleep. We've got a date in the morning with two good-looking guys!"

Long after Cissy's deep breathing signaled that she was in dreamland, Natalie lay awake, staring at the darkened ceiling. Her prayer, she now realized, had been as much for herself as for Cissy. Maybe she was more like the older girl than she knew. Oh, she didn't care about being in the limelight, but she sure wished she knew what God had in mind for the rest of her life. And even though she wanted to do His will, there was plenty of room for error, because her own "wanter" was working overtime. Right now, for example—just as Cissy had half-jokingly confessed about Antonio—Natalie wanted Scott to like her more than any other girl.

With this thought running around in her head, Natalie was about to drop off to sleep when she heard a muffled sound through the wall behind her headboard. Her eyes flew open and she listened again. The sound seemed to be coming from the room next door, where two of the finalists—Kameko and Courtney—and their chaperone were staying.

Yes! There it was again. Someone was sobbing. . . .

Nine

Ice skating should be just the thing to cool her disappointment over the competition, Cissy thought when she woke the next morning in the double bed next to Natalie. She could put it behind her, once and for all, and get on with her life. It didn't hurt any to know that she would be spending time with her cousin, his friend, and that gorgeous guy, Antonio, either.

"Did you hear anything last night?" Natalie wanted to know when she came out of the bathroom later.

"Are you kidding? I slept like a rock. Did you?"

The younger girl looked concerned. "Yeah. I think someone was crying in the room next to ours. Whoever it was, was really upset."

Cissy was about to ask about it when the phone rang. It was Antonio, waiting in the atrium downstairs, and there was no time to do anything but grab their coats and caps and take off for Scott's suite.

Her mom and Aunt Helen were getting ready to do some Christmas shopping when Cissy and Natalie stopped by. Elizabeth glanced at her and then in the mirror as she fastened her earrings. "When were you planning to use your gift certificate, honey?"

"Oh, I don't know . . . later this afternoon probably."

"Fine!" her mom said, a little too brightly. "Then
your Aunt Helen and I will scout out the bargains this
morning and save you some time later on."

Was that sympathy in Mom's tone? Cissy glanced
sharply at her mother's reflection, but Elizabeth
avoided her gaze and was busy scrambling for her
purse.

*She probably thinks I dread running into the models at
Macy's after losing last night. Well, she's right.* Most of
the finalists would be doing their shopping today, before returning to their hometowns. Cissy felt another
twinge of regret. It would be tough going back to Garden City empty-handed. But . . . suppose she returned
with a new boyfriend?

A lot of her friends—the "in" crowd at Shawnee
High—had been envious when she'd dated Ron, who
was a college student last year while she was a senior
in high school. Wouldn't they just flip to know that Antonio Carlo had not only graduated from college but
had already embarked on a glamorous career?

"Scott, bring your camera," she ordered in a burst
of enthusiasm. "I want to be sure to get a picture of
Antonio and me."

"Hey, cuz, what's your problem? You didn't like the
one I took of you two in the hallway?"

Surprised at his brusque tone, Cissy's mouth
dropped open. Natalie, too, seemed to be wondering
what had happened to the best-natured guy around.
Elizabeth and Helen, shrugging into their coats, even
stopped to stare.

Eyeing Scott carefully, Cissy asked, "Uh . . . *what* picture in the hallway?"

"The one where you two *fell* for each other. Antonio, wallowing on the floor. You, leaning against the wall and holding your eye, blood dripping off your hand. Ha!" he said triumphantly, pointing at the look of dawning awareness on Cissy's face. "Gotcha!"

They were all laughing by then. Elizabeth buttoned her camel hair coat. "Are you really falling for Antonio, Cissy?"

"Looks promising," she confessed with a grin.

"Then you'd better wear your White Dove necklace today." Scott slanted a meaningful look in Cissy's direction.

"Oops!" She felt for the silver chain. "I seem to have left it in the room. Can I borrow yours, Scott?"

"I *need* mine!" he objected forcefully.

Cissy let out an involuntary little squeak, then covered her mouth with her hand. At the questioning look on the women's faces, she noticed that Natalie had sunk into one of the plush chairs, picked up a magazine, and became really absorbed in reading.

Scott blushed all the way to his hairline. Everyone knew—at least the kids in Natalie's church did—that the little white dove many of them were either wearing as jewelry or carrying in their pockets was a symbol of their commitment to purity. The movement had begun as a pledge to sexual abstinence before marriage, but Nat's youth group had taken it much further to include total purity in all areas of life, including putting Christian love into action.

Cissy watched her cousin grimace, then press the

heel of his hand to his forehead. "What I *mean* is, I haven't talked to Antonio yet about . . . spiritual things. He knows where I stand, but I need to say something—if I get a chance—so I carry the dove keychain with me as a reminder. . . ." Scott's words trailed off weakly.

Cissy grinned. She knew what he'd been thinking. When the white doves were mentioned, everyone's first thought was S-E-X. He gave a gesture of helplessness, and she winked at him. "Go get your camera, Scott."

Totally clueless, Mom and Aunt Helen gave Scott a fond smile and waggled their fingers as they left the room. But Natalie's head was still buried in her magazine!

~===~

Accompanying the happy chatter of people hurrying about the atrium was the melody of "The Twelve Days of Christmas." Funny how the Christmas countdown seemed to start earlier every year, Cissy thought.

Scott snapped a picture of her and Antonio against the backdrop of a glittering tree, then had Antonio take one of him and Natalie.

On their way out of the building, Antonio looked up, listening. "Did you know that number is supposed to have been inspired by an old drinking song?"

"You've done some research?" Cissy jested feebly, although she was a little worried. Drinking was nothing to joke about. She ought to know—with *their* family history.

"On music . . . or drinking?" Antonio grinned. "I read somewhere that instead of 'A partridge in a pear tree,' the words used to be, 'A pie sat on a pear tree.'"

"Huh! The songwriter must have been drunk at the time," Scott quipped.

Thankfully, with the overnight temperature drop, the conversation soon turned to the weather.

"Think it's going to snow?" Natalie asked from the backseat of Antonio's sports car.

He glanced at her in the rearview mirror. "Wouldn't be surprised. It's cold enough. It's a good thing you guys brought some warm clothing."

Cissy felt a delicious little shiver at the look he gave her. She was glad she'd thought to pack her white ski jacket with the blue turtleneck that brought out her eyes. And Scott and Natalie were bundled up in parkas and knit caps. For a few seconds, there was nothing but the honking of horns and the blowing of whistles in the busy street. Cissy wondered if the others were thinking about all the homeless people out there—like Gertrude—who didn't have anything but a thin, buttonless coat to keep out the chill.

She brushed off that dismal thought and smiled at how well the four of them were getting along. Of course, Natalie always got along with everybody, and Scott was a great guy—even if he was her cousin. Looking over at Antonio, so strong and sure of himself in this crazy traffic, Cissy felt another little thrill. If Antonio Carlo was the consolation prize, then she was glad she'd lost!

She began to feel a little shaky, however, when they stood on the plaza and looked down on the skating rink. "I didn't realize we'd have an audience," she said, noting all the people thronging the esplanade with its colorful array of United Nations flags whipping in the breeze.

"Too late to back out now," Antonio said, taking her arm. "Let's get our gear."

"This may be the mistake of my life," Cissy admitted after the tall Italian had laced up her white skates. She cut her eyes toward the ice.

"Don't worry. I won't let you fall"—he had the good grace to turn slightly red—"that is, I won't let you fall *again*. I'm only a klutz on Tuesdays."

Still on the sidelines, she watched Natalie trying to balance on the single blade, arms outspread. Nat let out a screech when Scott grabbed hold, almost taking her down. "What about *us*?" he called warily.

Antonio shrugged. "You're on your own, buddy." Then he skated out onto the ice and executed a perfect figure-eight. "Besides, you've got each other," he yelled to them.

Scott grinned as if he could go for that, while Natalie rolled her eyes. "You two go ahead then," he told Antonio. "I'm going to take some pictures . . . in case we need to be able to identify the bodies later."

Antonio chuckled at that and held out his gloved hands toward Cissy. "Well, here goes." She teetered toward the edge of the ice, took his hands, and allowed him to tug her onto the frozen surface.

It was easier than she thought, with Antonio skating backward and pulling her along in a straight-ahead glide pattern. She was doing fine—even though she felt awkward—until he made a turn. "Ohhh," she wailed.

"Hang on! You're doing great!"

Pretty soon, he was holding only one hand as they skated, side by side, several turns around the rink. When she had the hang of it, Antonio led her back to the side, where Natalie and Scott were waiting.

Cissy was jubilant. "You're going to love it, Nat! It's like flying!"

"Your turn, Natalie." Antonio put her through the same paces, and Cissy watched, still panting from her workout. Nat looked really good out there, but then she was much more athletic.

When it was Scott's turn, he backed off. "No way am I holding hands with Antonio Carlo!"

With that, Scott took the ice, flailing and thrashing as he fought to stay on his feet. Cissy was sure he was going to land flat on his face, but he righted himself just in time to stumble in another direction. He looked like a marionette with the strings dangling out of control. There was a roar of laughter from spectators as one skate went one way, and the other in the opposite direction. But before he managed a full split, he pivoted smoothly, spread his arms in a flying eagle, and skated back to them.

"Scott, I could wring your neck!" Cissy scolded. "You had us scared out of our minds! I didn't know you could skate like that."

He ducked his head modestly. "Sorry about that, cuz. Dad used to take Zac and me to a rink when we lived in California. So I've had a little practice."

Natalie squinted at the good-looking guy, his parka pulled up to his chin, a red cap covering his ears. "You've been holding out on us, Scott. Is there anything you *can't* do?"

He only grinned and took her hand. Soon, the two couples were sailing along together on the ice as if they had been skating like this forever—until Scott unexpectedly pulled Natalie into a fancy turn.

"Scott!" she yelled. "Stop! We're going too fast!"

"Sorry! I can't seem to slow down. This ice is faster than the ice in Califor-r-r-rnia."

The next thing she knew, they were down, skidding across the surface on their bottoms and ending in a tangle of arms and legs on the sidelines. They lay there in a heap, neither one able to move.

There were grunts and groans—Natalie couldn't tell which one was making the most noise. But at least they'd survived the spill. They unwound themselves and lay, panting for breath, on the cold ground. Then they lifted their heads, nose to nose, and looked at each other.

Even through blurred vision, Natalie could see herself mirrored in those dark eyes, like melted chocolate. She felt a tingling sensation that had nothing to do with her current crop of aches and bruises.

"You okay, Nat?"

She nodded. "I . . . I think so."

"Have I ever told you—"

She held her breath. Maybe *this* was where he'd tell her he liked her better than Katlyn Chander—or that he didn't.

But just at that moment, Cissy and Antonio skated over. "You guys okay?"

Antonio helped Natalie up, but Scott still lay there. "Except for my broken leg." He pushed himself up off the ice with his arms and winced.

"Oh, Scott," Natalie moaned, "it's all my fault! I couldn't make that turn—"

"I'll live." He took Antonio's outstretched arm and hoisted himself up, then took off around the rink like a speed skater, laughing back at them.

Natalie shook her head. That guy! She'd never seen Scott Lambert like this—so laid back and loose. Oh, in the past—even during the worst times—she'd caught flashes of his natural good humor. But here in New York, he seemed happier and more outgoing than ever.

On the other hand, why shouldn't he be? He had a great new friend in Antonio and had sold some pictures to the *New York Times*. If that wasn't the ultimate stamp of approval on his plans to be a photographer, she didn't know what it would take.

———

"I hope you guys are going to be around for a while," Antonio said as they made their way back to his car after hot chocolate and sandwiches at a rinkside restaurant.

"I'd say about . . . seventy years or so," Scott quipped.

Antonio made a face. "Natalie, how'd you ever get mixed up with a guy like this?"

She shrugged. "Him? I never saw him before in my life."

Laughing, she and Scott piled into the backseat, where he pulled her close and whispered in her ear. "I'm glad you *did* get mixed up with me, Nat."

She opened her mouth, but nothing came out. Her gaze locked on his, all she could manage was a squeaky, "Me too."

Invigorated by the exercise, Cissy was feeling super

on the drive back to the hotel. Antonio pointed out the sights—Central Park, a row of fine shops, and the library, guarded by two huge stone lions—then turned onto Fifth Avenue so they could get a look at the gold-plated front of Trump Towers.

Everything was great until Scott dropped the bomb. "Antonio, why do you think Cissy wasn't a winner in the Top Ten contest?"

Cissy cringed. *Scott, you jerk! Why bring up that subject?* She couldn't bear to look at Antonio but swiveled her head to stare out the window.

"I can't really say," Antonio began, maneuvering the little car through the heavy traffic. "There are certain qualities the judges look for. With the thirteen-year-old, it was probably her age. She has many years ahead as a model. Ardath had an unusual, exotic look about her. And Selena had no prior training, and that's a plus for runway modeling. It means she can be trained any way the designer wants, without having to undo years of learned habits."

Then he turned to Cissy, and she squirmed, still unable to look him in the eye. "You seemed so content with your life—win or lose—not necessarily the most desirable quality for a modeling career, Cissy. But I can't read the judges' minds. As far as I'm concerned, you *should* have won."

She basked in the glow of his compliment, then—she just had to ask. "Do you think it was . . . my eye . . . that kept me from winning?"

"Not at all. If anything, it made you more intriguing. I think everyone knew it was a wound that would heal."

"Speaking of wounds that heal—" And Scott was telling him about Katlyn Chander and how she'd turned her mishap into an advantage and had even become homecoming queen—the first wheelchair-bound queen in the history of Shawnee High!

Natalie felt her stomach knot up—the way it did every time Katlyn was mentioned. Now Scott was emphasizing God's part in the incident—for Antonio's benefit probably—and how He'd saved Katlyn's life. "God's always with us, you know."

Yes! And so is Katlyn Chander! Natalie griped to herself.

Cissy turned in her seat to look over her shoulder. "Did you know Katlyn's decided to become a psychologist, Nat?"

"No . . . I didn't." She dreaded what was sure to come next.

And it did. "What about you, Natalie?" Antonio asked casually, as if it was just any old question. "What are your career plans?"

She tried to stay cool. "Oh . . . I haven't decided."

"Natalie is one of those people who can do anything they set their minds to," Cissy said with a laugh. "You know . . . the most-likely-to-succeed type."

Scott reached over and squeezed her hand as if he agreed. But Natalie wondered why in the world she hadn't come up with something definite. Dad always said she was still young and had plenty of time to make up her mind. But most high school seniors had *some* idea what they wanted to do with their lives. *She* hadn't a clue.

As soon as Scott opened the door to the suite, his mom motioned the three of them inside. "We've had some excitement while you were out."

Natalie and Cissy followed slowly, question marks on both their faces. Helen Lambert and Elizabeth Stiles looked awful, Natalie thought—like they had seen a ghost or something.

"One of the contestants . . . tried to kill herself this morning . . . tried to jump over the balcony railing," Helen Lambert rasped out.

"Wh-what?!" All three mouths dropped open, and Natalie had visions of some poor girl bolting over the side and plunging thirty-seven floors to the atrium lobby below.

"Who was it?" Cissy wanted to know.

Natalie could see that Cissy was deathly pale, her complexion almost as white as her jacket.

"It was Kameko, honey. Here, sit down," her mother said gently, leading her to the couch, Scott and Natalie right behind. "This is a shock, I know. It was to all of us."

"Is she . . . is Kameko . . ."

"She's fine," Helen Lambert spoke up quickly. "That is, she isn't physically harmed. Someone stopped her before she could jump. But she's under observation in the psychiatric wing of one of the hospitals here. They'll keep her until her parents can get here. They didn't come with her from Hawaii, you know . . . the distance, I suppose."

Scott's mother broke down, and his aunt took over. Cissy was staring, glassy-eyed. "Apparently Kameko was quite depressed even before she arrived . . . and then not winning anything during the competition . . ." She looked away from her daughter's stricken expression, as if realizing what she had just said.

"Poor Kameko . . ." Cissy's voice sounded unnaturally thin and tight, like it might break any minute. "Of all the girls, she was the shyest. I didn't get to know her very well . . . I should have—"

"Hey, cuz," Scott cut in, "don't beat yourself. Who knows what makes people pull dumb stunts like that."

"We know only that she comes from a troubled family," his mom said. "Some kind of financial problem . . . and the marriage is not very stable. . . ."

Natalie felt for the woman. This had to be awful for the Stileses and the Lamberts, bringing back all kinds of nightmares. They'd had plenty of family troubles. Somebody had to say something, so she took the lead. "I remember thinking how sad—or scared—Kameko looked that first day . . . in the hospitality suite. She was hanging out with Ardath and Courtney. As a matter of fact"—it came to her then—Kameko was rooming right next door to Cissy!—"I think I heard her crying last night. . . ."

There was a deafening silence. What else was there to say?

When the phone rang, everyone jumped. Mrs. Lambert got there first. "Hello? Yes, of course. We'll get a cab and be there as soon as possible."

When she cradled the receiver, her face was drained. "That was Maria Carlo . . . at General Hospital. Kameko is asking for Cissy."

Ten

Cissy was stunned. "Me?" Feeling a little panicky, she turned to Natalie. "What could I possibly say to her?"

"You won't know till you get there." How did Nat always seem to come up with the right answer? "Or maybe you won't have to say anything at all. Maybe she just needs to talk."

It was decided that Scott and Natalie would go along to keep Cissy company, while the two women waited in the suite. "I'm sure she doesn't need that many visitors right now," her mom wisely determined. "And we probably wouldn't be able to see her anyway."

On the drive over, Cissy and the others were subdued, wondering what they would find when they got there. Cissy was doing some fast praying, too. Somehow it seemed easier to give her testimony in front of hundreds than to confront one person in crisis. What if she only made things worse?

Inside the huge hospital complex, a stressed-out receptionist in the lobby frowned when they told her who they wanted to see.

"The Psych Ward doesn't usually allow anyone but family to visit patients . . . but since the parents aren't here. . . ." A quick call confirmed that Cissy was expected and would be able to see Kameko—for fifteen minutes only—but that Scott and Natalie would have to remain in the upstairs waiting room.

Following directions to the Psychiatric Ward, they headed down a maze of hallways to an elevator. Stepping out on the ninth floor, they spotted a lounge area adjacent to a heavy barred door.

The Carlos, with Antonio right behind them, hurried to greet them. "We notified the girl's parents, and they're taking the next flight out of Honolulu," Maria told them. "Then we arranged to have Kameko brought here. But she refuses to be sedated until she's seen you, Cissy. She wouldn't even talk to Min Collins, her chaperone."

Cissy could see a look of bewilderment pass between the Carlos. "Has she told you what's wrong?"

"She won't tell us *anything*." Tomas was grim. "She insisted on seeing you first."

Cissy was taken to a wardenlike attendant, who grilled her like some criminal before allowing her to pass. "Only one visitor," he warned, holding up a beefy hand to halt Scott and Natalie in their tracks.

There was time for only a quick hug. "Pray for me, you guys," she whispered, then turned to step through. There was an awful feeling of finality when the metal door clanged shut behind her. She sincerely hoped the Lord would fill her in on what to say when the time came.

Cissy found Kameko in a small, padded room with a mattress, nothing else. She was wearing only a short hospital gown, her bare feet drawn up under her. Dull eyes peeked out—like chips of coal—through her black bangs.

"Kameko? It's Cissy Stiles. How are you feeling?"

The girl stared straight ahead, as if she hadn't heard. There was no chair, so Cissy sat on the floor beside her.

"Kameko, I'm here because I heard you wanted to see me. Is there anything I can do to help?"

The glazed eyes cleared a little. "Cissy? Is it you? You really came?"

"Of course, Kameko. I want to help . . . if I can."

Kameko pulled away, putting as much distance between herself and Cissy as she could manage on the mat. "No one can help. *No* one. I've failed."

"Then that makes two of us. I've failed, too. I didn't win the contest, either, you know. But that doesn't mean I'll be going back to my hometown a loser."

Cissy waited while the message sank in. The girl perked up a little. "You won't? Wh-what do you mean?"

"I have Someone who helps me every time I need Him."

Kameko dropped her head. "Then you're lucky. I don't have a boyfriend. I don't have . . . anyone."

Cissy shook her head. "I wasn't talking about a boyfriend. I'll tell you all about it. But first, I want to know what made you try . . . to hurt yourself. Was it losing the contest?"

Kameko made no sound, but Cissy could see two big tears well up in her eyes and start to trickle down the smooth cheeks. "It's more than that. Much more."

For the next few minutes, Kameko told about her father's drinking, the battering, the drunken rages. Now he had been laid off from his job and was threatening to leave them. "I am the only child . . . so it is up to me to do something. I . . . I thought that if I could win the $10,000, he would not have to drink to forget his troubles . . . and my parents would love each other again. But I failed!"

The girl was sobbing now, and Cissy reached over to touch her shoulder. "No, Kameko, you haven't failed. Obviously, they care very much—about *you*. They're on their way right now . . . to New York . . . together."

Kameko looked up in amazement. "But how? There was no money."

"I have an idea some . . . friends . . . helped." The Carlos! It had to be the Carlos. Yet she wasn't even sure they were believers. *God provides in some mysterious ways,* she thought. "Kameko . . . I know a little about the kind of trouble you've been having . . . except it was the wife who had a problem with alcohol."

Quickly, Cissy poured out her Aunt Helen's sad story and how it had affected the whole family—eventually even causing a terrible accident. Kameko listened to every word, latching on to the happy ending—Aunt Helen's recovery, Zac's community service, especially the part where Katlyn was elected homecoming queen.

Cissy reached up and unclasped her silver chain with the little dove pendant. Then she took Kameko's hand and placed it inside, closing her fingers around it. "Remember I told you I had Someone who watches over me? I'd like to tell you about Him. . . ."

Cissy seemed exhausted, Natalie thought, but she was positively glowing when the attendant unlocked the barred door and let her out.

"Kameko's sleeping now," Cissy told them. "The nurse was giving her a sedative when I left, so she'll probably be out the rest of the night." She filled them in on the details, then mentioned that she needed to call her mother and Aunt Helen.

Tomas Carlo, looking vastly relieved, put his hand on her arm. "When you reach them, tell them to join us at the agency—that is, if you don't have other plans. There's something we need to discuss—with your entire family."

When his cousin was out of sight, Scott let out a sigh. "Whew! I'd love to have been a fly on the wall in there."

All three of the Carlos swiveled their heads to stare at him. Natalie wondered why. Hadn't they ever heard that expression before? Maybe not—way up here in the north.

By the time they reached the agency on Herald Square, the sky was overcast, and a raw wind was gusting through the streets, thick with holiday shoppers. Cissy barely noticed the weather *or* the traffic. She was planning how she should phrase her response to the offer the Carlos were about to make her. Why else would they have called this unexpected meeting . . . on top of the tragedy that could have ruined the agency's reputation forever! She shivered inside her down jacket, as much from anticipation as from the cold.

Inside, Tomas Carlo switched on some flexible

overhead lights, then trained them on a table, where dozens of photos were spread out.

"Thank you for coming, ladies." He acknowledged her mom and aunt. "I thought you'd want to be here for this announcement."

Cissy's heart raced—at about the same speed Antonio's presence produced. She rehearsed her lines: *I can't tell you how much I appreciate this offer. . . .*

"We haven't had much time to think of anything but the competition all week," Tomas began, "compounded by the unfortunate incident this morning." He cleared his throat. "But Antonio insisted we take a look at these. And, frankly, Maria and I were astounded—both by the photos and by our son's perception." He flashed Antonio a dazzling smile.

Antonio gave a mock bow and motioned to the group to step up and have a look. Not wanting to crowd in, Cissy stood back with Natalie while the others moved forward.

"Oh, my!" Aunt Helen was the first to react. It was as if she couldn't believe her eyes.

"These are really fantastic," her mom agreed.

The Carlos were beaming, but nobody in Cissy's family cracked a smile. They appeared stunned. Scott, especially.

Maria explained. "In this business, we're trained to recognize model potential wherever we find it—young, old, male, female. Antonio has the knack, too. He spotted the talent here right away and has been taking these pictures"—she gestured toward the table—"since you people arrived last Tuesday afternoon. Although there was so much going on, he insisted we take a look. And we agree with him. This is a rare find—a unique photogenic quality we seldom see."

Cissy was getting nervous. Why were they making such a production out of this? Why not just tell her about the offer?

Aunt Helen and Elizabeth moved aside as Cissy and Natalie took their places in front of the light table. They looked at the photos—every one of them. Cissy was in a few, but the pictures clearly focused on one person—and one person alone. And that one person was not Cissy Stiles!

It's over now for sure, she thought. *The competition is really over.* While a part of her was really happy about this, another felt as if she'd taken a flying leap from the Empire State Building and hit bottom—with a thud.

God's purpose for her being in New York suddenly seemed perfectly clear.

So did Antonio Carlo's undivided attention.

This was not about *her* at all.

It was about . . . Scott!

He's the one who's going to get the offer!

What's going on? Natalie wondered. A scene straight out of *Sleeping Beauty?* Everyone in the room appeared to have been touched by the magic wand of the wicked witch and were suspended in time, their expressions frozen.

All heads had turned toward Scott, who looked like he was in a coma.

Antonio, with his head tilted to one side and wearing a mischievous dimple-making grin, could have been a mannequin in a department store window.

Cissy, totally dumbfounded and with her mouth hanging open, kept her gaze glued to her cousin.

Elizabeth Stiles gasped and covered her heart with one hand.

Helen Lambert's perfectly arched brows were drawn together in bewilderment, and she was biting her lower lip as if to keep it from trembling. *Could I be dreaming?* Natalie asked herself. But this was no dream. She was no beauty, and Prince Charming wasn't about to kiss her and wake her up. She felt as if she were in an entirely different play. . . . Maybe "somewhere over the rainbow." *Yes, that's it. I'm Dorothy from* The Wizard of Oz *. . . and I want to go home, where I belong. . . .*

It was Scott who finally broke the spell. He made a strange sound in his throat, like what he'd intended to say hadn't quite made it out of his mouth. "This is a joke, right?" he croaked. "You got me all right, big guy—really had me going there for a minute. . . ."

Antonio, arms folded over his chest, shrugged. "No joke, pal. Something like this is not my brand of humor. Anyway," he added, "my parents make the deals around here. I have nothing to do with that."

"The contract is in here." Tomas withdrew an envelope from his inside coat pocket. "Look it over, and if you have any questions—"

"Wait a minute. What contract? I'm no model," Scott protested, looking from the Carlos to his mom, who still appeared dazed.

"Think about it," Maria implored with a smile. "But we *will* need an answer before you leave New York. If you decide to accept, we'll need to start working on a portfolio right away."

<center>~~~</center>

"Have a hol-ly, jol-ly Christmas," drifted from the canned music in the hotel sound system when they returned and took the escalator. Cissy lifted her eyes all the way to the domed ceiling—forty-eight floors above. "Yeah—right!" she scoffed. "You know what, Nat? Some of us who model for Belk's used to laugh about being discovered by some scout at one of our fashion shows. But who would have ever thought it would happen like *this* . . . and to *Scott*!"

Natalie could understand Cissy's frustration. How ironic that her cousin, who couldn't care less, would be the one to land a contract. "Well . . ." she fumbled for words, "I guess it couldn't have happened to a nicer guy, anyway."

What Cissy didn't know was that Natalie could identify with the whole fiasco. Both of them were confused about the future: Cissy, with her growing doubts about modeling as a career; herself, with whether or not she and Scott *had* a future—together.

Well, that much seemed pretty obvious now. She'd known from the beginning that she and Scott had more against them than for them: his wealthy, society-conscious family—her middle-income, working-class one; his fantastic, star-quality good looks—her ordinary, nothing-special face and figure; his confidence about his career goals—her question marks. When she put it all together, she wondered how he'd put up with her this long. They were as different as night and day—and the gap was widening fast!

Nobody said anything about shopping or sight-seeing for the rest of the day. They all gathered in the suite, talking among themselves after each phone call that Helen and Elizabeth made—to Dr. Lambert, Scott's dad; John Stiles, Cissy's dad; their aunt, Martha Brysen, and eventually, the Lamberts' lawyer, who asked them to fax him a copy of the contract.

"Nobody is listening to me," Scott complained, jumping up from the couch, where he'd been sitting next to Natalie. "You guys are talking about me as if I'm not even in the room."

Cissy turned her big sky-blue eyes toward him. "It's the most fabulous offer in the world, Scott. Why wouldn't you be thrilled? *I* sure would be."

"I know you would, cuz," he said in a small voice. "And I'm sorry."

"Oh, I'm not blaming you . . . and I'm not mad. Really. But I'll have to admit it feels weird."

"You got it. It doesn't feel real. Besides"—he began to pace, flinging his arms out—"I can't be a model!"

"Why not?" Cissy seemed baffled.

"Because I'm more comfortable *behind* the camera than in *front* of it. I can't see myself standing around . . . posing." His voice trailed off and he ducked his head, looking embarrassed.

His mother sank into the nearest chair. "Your dad is still hoping you'll be a doctor, you know."

Scott's shoulders slumped and he let out a long sigh. "Well, I don't want to disappoint him, Mom. But I'm not cut out to be a doctor any more than I'm cut out to be a model. And then there's something else. If

I did this model thing, wouldn't it be kind of a joke? I can just see the other guys. I'd be laughed at!"

Cissy snorted. "Yeah . . . all the way to the bank! This is a world-famous agency we're talking about here, you know."

"I'll grant you that. But Antonio made those pictures when I didn't know what he was doing. I thought he was just taking some shots of the three of us—you know, for the old memory book. I wasn't posing. What if I couldn't do it?"

"It's your decision, Scott," his mom said. "But it wouldn't hurt to get the attorney's opinion of the contract. Why don't you run down and fax him a copy? Your dad will want to look at it, too. Then you can join us at the hotel restaurant for dinner—it's too late to get reservations anywhere else."

Natalie could see that Scott was reluctant, but he took the contract and folded it.

"Go with me, Nat?" He looked kind of pleading, she thought, like a little boy who wasn't sure what was going to happen next.

Frankly, Natalie was glad to get out of there. She needed some air. Her chest felt like it was weighted down with a ton of cement. *I've lost Scott,* she thought all the way to the mezzanine level, *before I could even find out if I had a chance with him.* She knew they had to go their separate ways after graduation—at least for a while. But it was happening too soon.

"What do you think of all this, Nat?" Scott asked on the elevator ride down.

Her heart had already hit bottom, but she had to tell the truth. "It's an opportunity of a lifetime," she admitted. "But like your mom said, it's got to be your decision. You have to feel right about it, Scott." She had an idea. "Why don't you ask yourself what you'd do if you *didn't* sign the contract."

"Hmmm." He looked thoughtful the rest of the way. Then, stepping out into the carpeted hallway, he led her over to a bench beneath one of the Christmas trees and motioned for her to sit down.

Scott sat beside her, rolled up the contract, and tapped it against his thigh. The tree lights winked and blinked, with a dizzying, almost hypnotic effect. What he said next could settle everything between them. "I've made up my mind, Nat,"—she waited, hardly able to breathe—"about photography. Jack Henderson wanting my photos really clenched that for me. He thinks I have a future in the business. So does Antonio. But there's *this* offer—"

Natalie couldn't keep quiet another minute. She gulped in a breath, then plunged in. "Yeah . . . not many people have to make a choice between *two* great careers."

"*If* I go the modeling route . . . that would only be a temporary deal." Natalie got the creepy sensation he was talking to himself more than to her. "I could still go on with my plans to train for photography . . . and maybe even pick up a few tips from the other side of the camera. . . ." Suddenly he seemed to remember she was sitting there. "But if I *do* sign, Nat, we might not end our senior year together."

She nodded, miserable with the direction this conversation was taking.

"The Carlos mentioned working up a portfolio right away. That means I could be called back to New York any time. You know, Mom's already mentioned that if we had to, we could get a tutor and I could take my finals and graduate with the class . . . or even afterward."

There was a long pause while they both thought it over. "Things happen for a reason, Scott," she said finally. Maybe the Lord knew it would be too tempting for her to be near Scott much longer. Right now, for example, she felt like throwing herself into his arms and begging him never to leave her!

"I believe that, too," he said softly, "including your being here with me in New York. What does it all mean, Nat?"

She shrugged. "I don't know. Maybe you just needed a sounding board . . . or a friend." Although she could hardly be an objective one. "My dad says the best thing to do when you have a major decision to make is to pray about it, then get busy with other things while you're listening for that still, small voice."

"Good advice. Well, first things first," he said, getting to his feet with an eager little spring to his step, she thought. "Guess I'd better get this contract faxed."

On the way to the registration desk, he apologized. "I'm sorry all this happened, Nat. I really wanted to show you a good time in New York." He grabbed her hand and gave it a little squeeze. "You're one in a million, and I don't want to lose you . . . but I've got to give this some serious thought—and prayer. Right now, I don't have a clue as to what I should do."

He knows it, too, she was thinking. *He knows this is the beginning of the end for us—whether he signs that contract . . . or not.*

Eleven

Natalie and Cissy had arranged for an early wake-up call so they'd have time to look at the Sunday paper before leaving for church. Jack Henderson's articles on Gertrude and Cissy—along with Scott's pix—were slated for the early-morning edition.

Natalie dressed in the black skirt and angora sweater, then waited by the window while Cissy gave her smooth page-boy hairstyle a final brushing.

Looking out, Natalie noticed that a cold rain had fallen during the night, and water puddled on the roof-tops of several low-lying buildings. Patches of blue brightened the wintry sky, and a pale sun shone on the upper stories of skyscrapers, lighting them with an incandescent glow. The lower stories were still draped in shadows. She figured that, in winter, the only time the sunlight reached some of the sidewalks was when the sun was shining directly overhead.

"Come look, Cissy."

Down below, row upon row of bright yellow taxi-cabs lined the streets as far as the eye could see. "I read about that." Cissy picked up her visitor's guide and flipped to the section on transportation. "It says there are 1,200 of the medallion Yellow Cabs in New York City." With a little giggle, she added, "I think I saw a taxi in Garden City—once!"

"Then you've seen about half the town's entire transportation system."

Laughing, they grabbed their coats, locked the door behind them, and headed for the Lamberts' suite.

Scott answered the door on the first knock. "Come on in. The articles are great!" They stood behind the couch, craning their necks over Helen's and Elizabeth's shoulders as they read the full-page spread. There was a picture of Cissy, with the caption—"Visiting Beauty Has Date With Death." Then the story of the homeless woman, illustrated by the pictures Scott had taken.

"We'll have to take Gertrude a copy," he said, looking pleased.

"We'll need *several* extra copies to take home." Helen Lambert was obviously pretty ecstatic. "You, too, Natalie. You're in this picture with Gertrude, and you're mentioned in both articles."

Natalie had scanned the article, subtitled "Teens With Integrity." What was the big deal? She'd just tagged along with Scott. And as far as she was concerned, neither one of them had done anything spectacular.

"When I called Tony to thank him for showing the photos to Jack," Scott was saying, "I invited him to go to church with us."

Natalie's blue eyes widened. So Scott was calling him "Tony" now!

"Well . . . is he?" Cissy asked, hope in her baby blues.

"Yep. Said he'd even pick us up and give us the grand tour of some other famous churches afterward. Seemed real eager to see us."

Elizabeth gave her daughter a knowing look. "As eager as Cissy—whenever that good-looking Italian's name is mentioned?"

"Give me a break, Mom!" Cissy cocked her head and braced her arms on her hips. "I was just thinking what a waste it would be if we didn't hail one of those 1,200 cabs waiting out on the street."

Natalie laughed, but the others looked blank, not having the foggiest idea what she was talking about.

"Well, I must say I'm glad to see you showing a little interest in someone again, honey. You haven't dated since Ron. . . ."

"Oh, I like Antonio, Mom," Cissy admitted. "But it's pretty obvious that all this time, it wasn't *me* he was after. He was simply courting a prospective talent." She gave Scott a scorching look, then batted at him playfully.

"Whoa!" Scott put up his hands in self-defense. "I'm already taken. I'm being courted by someone who's a whole lot prettier than Antonio." He winked at Natalie. "She followed me all the way to New York."

"Scott!" Natalie blushed and felt her heart sprout wings, then crash-dive at her next thought. *That's got to be a joke.*

As if to confirm her opinion, Elizabeth and Helen merely laughed off the remark and reached for their coats. Even the background music joined in the mockery as they rode down to the lobby on the elevator. "I'll . . . be home . . . for Christmas. You . . . can count . . . on me. . . ."

145

I'll be home for Christmas, Natalie reminded herself. *But . . . where will Scott be?*

"Can we all fit in your car?" Cissy asked when they met Antonio in the atrium, recalling that it had been a tight squeeze for Natalie and Scott in the backseat of his sports car.

The sudden light that sparked his dark eyes made her wonder if he was thinking what she was thinking— that it wouldn't be half bad, being wedged in together like that.

But he only shrugged it off, although that intriguing little dimple popped up beside his mouth. "I brought Dad's car." He motioned past the area where the cabs and limos were waiting for their next fares. "I'm parked across the street."

Outside, Antonio fell into step beside Cissy, then took her arm, steering her around the hotel attendants pushing luggage carts and the people getting in and out of vehicles. "Watch out for those puddles," he cautioned, then led the entourage to the long Lincoln Towncar parked on the other side of the street.

On the way, he leaned down and whispered in Cissy's ear. "I'm glad Scott asked me along."

She tilted her face up at him—a real treat. Most guys were shorter than she. Antonio towered over her. She liked that. She liked everything she knew about Antonio. Still, she reminded herself that Scott hadn't signed that contract yet. Antonio might just be "doing his job."

A little later, sitting beside her in the pew at The

Cathedral of Saint John the Divine, he seemed perfectly at ease and attentive during the Protestant worship hour.

"The building is still unfinished, although services have been held here since 1899," Antonio said afterward when they stood admiring the French Gothic architecture.

"Did the church run out of money?" Natalie put in.

Antonio grinned, his teeth dazzling against his olive skin. "No, nothing like that. They shut down voluntarily to make the point that it was more important to help the poor. In fact, part of the fame of this church is that its building is still incomplete. But there's another building around here you really ought to see," he spoke briskly as they left the sanctuary. "Saint Patrick's."

"Oh yes." Elizabeth whipped out her tourist guide. "I understand that one's a must."

Soon, they were all gawking at the twin spires that rose 330 feet high. The decorative bronze doors at the main entrance were outstanding, as well as the huge bronze altar inside.

"And just look at those stained-glass windows," Helen remarked in a hushed tone.

Antonio reeled off some more information. "If you measured it, you'd find that this cathedral is the length of a football field and is constructed in the shape of a Latin cross."

Cissy was impressed. "How do you know all this?"

"Goes with the territory, I suppose. I took Art History. Then, just being a native of New York helps. This is not the first unofficial tour I've conducted, you know," he joked. "I've brought other models here on a swing through the city."

The women walked ahead to examine some of the statuary down front, and Cissy noticed that Scott dropped back, so she was in hearing distance when he asked, as if it were the most normal thing in the world, "Hey, Tony, are you a Christian?"

Since she really wanted to hear what he had to say, she hung around. He answered right away. "I believe in God. Who doesn't?"

"That's not what I'm asking, Tony. I'm asking if Jesus Christ is your Lord and Savior."

To Cissy's horror, Antonio froze up, the dark eyes glittering. "I'd say that's a pretty personal matter, chum. Don't push it."

He strode off toward the chancel, leaving Cissy, Scott, and Natalie to stare after him in bewilderment.

"Whew!" Scott whistled between his teeth. "This may have been the place, but it obviously wasn't the right time to bring up that subject!"

But when Antonio walked back up the aisle, all smiles, with Scott's mom and aunt each clinging to an arm, Scott muttered under his breath, "The guy sure knows how to turn on the charm, I'll say that for him. Guess all we can do now is pray."

"How about a bite of the Big Apple?" Antonio asked as if the other little scene had never taken place. "I heard you say you'd like to do some sightseeing. If you don't have any other plans, I'd love to show you around." He looked right past Scott to Cissy, who was still numb.

She couldn't help it. A little shiver of excitement

stirred. He might not be a believer, but what harm could a few hours do? It wasn't as if she were going to marry the guy!

Scott shrugged. "I'm game."

"Ladies?" Antonio lifted one dark brow, giving them all a sweeping glance, but Cissy felt his gaze linger on her—almost like a caress.

Aunt Helen was the first to speak up. "Well, Elizabeth, how could we turn down such a charming offer?"

⸺

The afternoon flew by, beginning with lunch at a popular soul food restaurant in Harlem.

"I've been converted!" Elizabeth smacked her lips over the delicious food.

Cissy rolled her eyes. "If the Garden Club ladies could only see you now!"

After blackberry cobbler—as good as any they'd tried on trips to the South—Antonio suggested a walking tour of the area.

"But isn't it too dangerous?" the women wanted to know.

"If you don't know where you're going, it could be. But you'll be with me." He gave them his most convincing grin. But when they paired off, Cissy clung to his arm, glancing about a little fearfully.

They had spotted some slums from the car windows, but when they began their tour, Antonio pointed out the beautiful mansions and town houses built around 1900 at Sugar Hill. They stopped by Apollo Theater, where famous musicians got their start. Then they toured the colorful outdoor markets and souvenir shops on 125th Street.

Scott was clearly impressed. "All I ever knew about Harlem was that it's the home of the Globetrotters."

"And the homeless," Natalie added.

"Yeah. . . ." Scott appeared thoughtful. "That reminds me—we really ought to check on Gertrude before we leave New York."

Antonio glanced at his watch. "There's just so much to see and do—and so little time. Some places—like the Metropolitan Museum of Art and the United Nations complex—could take a full day. But no trip to New York is complete without a visit to the Statue of Liberty. If we hurry, we could make the late-afternoon ferry."

The boat ride over to Ellis Island was enchanting, Natalie thought, seeing the rays of the dying sun glancing off the choppy waves. She huddled in her parka until Scott took pity on her and put his arm around her. She noticed that Antonio and Cissy were doing the same, along with the two women. But none of them wanted to miss a minute of this view of the city skyline.

Lady Liberty herself was magnificent, standing tall and proud in New York Harbor. And on the island, Natalie leaned over to read the inscription on the plaque at the base: "Give me your tired, your poor, your huddled masses yearning to breathe free. Send these, the homeless, tempest-tossed, to me."

"Sounds a little like Jesus' invitation to the world, doesn't it?" Scott said, waiting until Antonio was out

of earshot. "Except that His brand of freedom is forever."

"Yeah," Natalie sighed. "No slums or alleys in
heaven."

Antonio called out to them then, and they climbed
the circular stairway leading to the head of the statue.
When they reached the top, gasping for breath, he gestured toward the great view. "There she is—the most
exciting city in the world. You've only barely gotten acquainted. Next time, you'll have to stay longer."

Natalie felt a sinking sensation. Scott and the others would be back—probably many times. But she had
an idea there would be no "next time" for her. She
drank in the sight—just as the sun slipped below the
horizon—storing up the memory of tall buildings and
lights blinking on . . . and Scott's strong profile, sil-
houetted in the growing darkness.

On Sunday night, after a late supper—they'd
stopped by the hospital to check on a beaming Kameko, who was being released to return to Hawaii with
her parents—everyone split up to turn in early. With
only one day left, they all needed some down time.

Cissy still had her shopping to do, and Natalie—
well, until she got home to Garden City, there was always the hope that Scott would tell her how he really
felt about her.

In their room, Cissy took off her shoes and plopped
back against her pillow. "My feet are killing me! We
must have walked ten miles today!"

"At least." Natalie massaged her own aching feet

while they lay there, too tired to get up and get ready for bed. She was feeling a little sad. It would soon be over. So much had happened—she would never forget a single minute of any of it. But there were still a lot of unanswered questions. Cissy had been reflective, too. "What do you make of what happened in the cathedral today, Nat?" she asked now. "That thing with Scott and Antonio. . . ."

Natalie thought about it. "I don't think Antonio knows he *needs* to be saved. He has everything already—money, looks, education, a good job waiting for him. It's all there—on a silver platter."

Cissy made a soft little sound. Natalie figured she was thinking that about described *her.* "But that's the toughest kind of person to reach—somebody who thinks he—or she—can handle anything—at least anything money can buy. But it doesn't work that way."

A long silence stretched out. Only the faint sound of another Christmas carol could be heard through the heavy door. Natalie knew Cissy was thinking of her family—the hard times that had brought them closer together—and to God. That's why she was a little surprised when Cissy burst out laughing.

"I was just remembering what we used to call Aunt Martha—*Saint* Martha! And it was no compliment in those days. We all thought she was bananas, a real fanatic."

Natalie chuckled along with her at the thought of Elizabeth Stiles and Helen Lambert's sweet-faced older sister, Martha Brysen, a staunch member of Natalie's church and now an outspoken advocate for the White Dove campaign. She *deserved* sainthood after all her family had put her through!

"Even though this is Sunday, Cissy, I don't feel like I've had a minute all day just to talk to God . . . by myself. Want to do it right now . . . together? We could pray for Scott and Antonio."

Cissy sat up, crossed her legs, and patted the bed beside her. "Come on over."

Holding hands, they prayed—Cissy first, then Natalie. "And, Lord, give us all patience to wait for your perfect will. Amen."

There was a moment of silence while they thought over the events of the day. "Antonio gave Scott a real challenge today, didn't he?" Cissy said as she unfolded her long legs and grabbed her boxers and T-shirt on her way to the bathroom.

Natalie nodded. "I have an idea that's not the end of it. Scott won't let it rest." *Even if he has to sign that contract. . . .*

Her thoughts were interrupted by the jangling of the telephone on the nightstand. It was Scott. "Sure. Sounds great. See you in the morning." She hung up, halfway to heaven. Breakfast at seven-thirty—for *two.* Maybe it wasn't too late. Maybe he'd saved the best for last!

They had just dropped off to sleep when the phone rang again. Cissy fumbled for the receiver. "Hello?"

It was a breathless Scott. "I called the shelter. Gertrude's missing!"

Twelve

"Missing?" Cissy was still groggy. "Who . . . what's missing? Here, Nat, maybe you can make some sense out of this. Scott's talking crazy." She handed over the phone and slumped back onto the pillow.

Natalie came to instantly. "What is it, Scott?"

She listened while he filled her in. A telephone call to check on Gertrude had turned up the alarming news that the little gray-haired woman hadn't been seen since the middle of the afternoon. And in these freezing temperatures. . . . The police had been called in, of course, and he'd asked Tony to help look for her.

"Be there in five minutes, Scott."

Natalie dressed in a hurry, then roused Cissy long enough to tell her where she was going and hear a mumbled response. Had she heard correctly?

Not taking time to ask, she did as she was told— grabbed Cissy's down jacket—and raced around the hallway to Scott's door.

He opened at her first light rap, finger to his lips. "Shhh. Mom and Aunt Liz have crashed." He stepped out into the hallway and carefully pulled the door shut behind him, shrugging into his heavy coat. "They'd

154

freak out if they knew we were going out on the streets this time of night. But I left them a note—in case one of them wakes up and wonders where I am. Let's go. Tony said he'd be waiting for us out front."

They walked, noiselessly, down the deserted corridor toward the elevator and descended with a whoosh toward the atrium. The lobby was a little more subdued now, though the late-night crowd in the bar was just getting cranked up. New York City at midnight was a whole new world.

Outside, a blast of frigid air whistled around the corner of the building. Natalie pulled her hood up over her head and snuggled into the bundle she'd brought along.

At the curb, Antonio was waiting in his sports car. Spotting them, he signaled them over and started the engine. "We'd better check the shelter first and find out what the police are doing about this, if anything." Natalie thought he seemed skeptical. "One homeless person on a busy holiday weekend. . . ." No need to say more.

The shelter was located in a pretty rough neighborhood—trashed alleyways and dark corners where streetlights had been shot out. The scene reminded her of mysteries she'd read. She half expected to see a murder—or at least a mugging—right before her eyes.

The people at the shelter weren't very encouraging. They were up to their eyeballs in new admissions. "The weather, you know," said the harried woman at the front desk. "They come in off the streets when it's really cold like this."

"But did the old lady—Gertrude—say anything to anyone about why she might be leaving . . . or where she'd go?" Scott persisted.

"How would *I* know?" She shrugged, impatient. "I wasn't on duty this afternoon, and the day shift people have all gone home."

"Mind if we ask around?"

"Help yourself." She peered over her glasses just as the door burst open with a blast of icy wind, and a drunk stumbled in. "Next."

The woman had already forgotten about them, Natalie decided as she trailed behind Scott and Antonio. They started with a man who appeared to be about Gertrude's age, and Antonio whipped out a clipping from the morning *Times*. "Have you seen this woman around here today?"

The man squinted through dirty glasses. "Nope. Can't say that I have."

They moved on, passed up a couple of women who were fighting over a blanket, and stopped by an open door. Inside, a young woman with tangled blond hair was sitting on a cot, holding a sleeping baby. She smiled when she saw them and motioned them in.

"Sure glad to have a roof over our heads tonight. My baby and me—we've been sleepin' under the Bridge till this front blew in. My man—he run off and left us in his daddy's truck."

"That's too bad, ma'am," Scott said, genuinely sympathetic. "We were wondering . . . have you seen this woman?"

The blonde looked at the photo in the newspaper, then at Natalie. "That you in that picture?"

Natalie nodded. "We're worried about the little old lady. She's out in the weather, and we need to find her. It would sure help us to know if you've seen or talked to her today."

The woman laid the baby on the cot and covered her with a corner of the tattered blanket. "Matter of fact, I did. Said she was tired of waitin' for the caseworker, and she'd make out just fine by herself. Said she wanted to find some 'new friends' before they got outta town. . . ."

Scott snapped his fingers. "That's it! I think I know where she may have gone! Thanks, ma'am, thanks a lot—and I hope everything works out just fine for you."

Antonio looked surprised but followed Scott out the door, Natalie right behind.

"Herald Square," he shouted above the wind. "I think she may be in the alley beside the Top Ten building—where Nat and I found her."

Antonio didn't hesitate. "Come on! Let's go!"

It didn't take long to find the tiny figure, huddled next to a stray mongrel inside her cardboard box in the alleyway. "Meet my new friend, P-Patches," Gertrude mumbled through chattering teeth. "He's been keepin' me warm . . . till you come. Knowed ya would. Just had to see ya one more time 'fore ya left."

It was all Natalie could do to hold back the tears. "Here, Gertrude." She wrapped Cissy's down jacket around the thin frame—dog and all. The coat flopped down to the old woman's knees. "It's an early Christmas present . . . from a friend you haven't met yet."

They didn't have too much trouble persuading Gertrude to return to the shelter. "Just so long as they take Patches, too," she insisted. "Kept me from freezin', ya know."

They left her there—beaming that snaggle-toothed grin and clutching Patches and the newspaper clippings—with the promise to see her tomorrow.

Make that later today, Natalie amended silently with an exhausted sigh.

⟤⟤⟤

Still too hyped to go to sleep anytime soon, after Antonio dropped them off at the front door of the hotel, Scott and Natalie found the coffee shop. "How about a *real* early breakfast?" he suggested.

"Maybe some hot chocolate and a Danish."

When the waitress brought their order, they sipped their hot drinks in silence, listening to the dreamy music of a dance band in the lounge next door. The coffee shop of a fancy hotel in New York City—after midnight. What could be more romantic than that?

Then Scott got right to the point. "Funny how things hardly ever turn out the way you think they're going to."

Yeah. Hardly ever. Natalie groaned inwardly. *Here it comes*.

"I've been wanting to talk to you all week, Nat. Now, especially. . . ." She waited for the other shoe to drop. "If I sign that contract, I won't be going back on the plane with the rest of you. The agency wants me to stay and begin work on my portfolio . . . now."

For a minute, she couldn't bring herself to say a word. "Well, in a few months, all us seniors will be going our separate ways." She picked at a crumb of Danish on her plate. "You just started sooner than the rest of us, that's all. You already have a great career underway."

"You mean . . . modeling?"

She nodded.

"I don't see that as any long-term thing, Natalie. I just happened to be in the right place at the right time.

In fact, I hear that most models don't last very long."
He grinned and touched his thick hair. "Who knows,
I may even go bald in the next few years—and this
time, it won't be on purpose!"

Natalie laughed, remembering when he'd shaved
his head—then winced, remembering *why*. Katlyn
again! He'd shaved his head because Katlyn had dared
Natalie to do it and prove that "beauty was more than
skin deep." It had been a really noble thing for Scott
to do, and Natalie loved him for it. In fact, she loved
him—period.

"You were great to try to help Katlyn like that, Scott.
That accident was terrible for her . . . in some ways."
Natalie shook off the nightmarish memory. "But maybe
that's what it took to help her see she needed the Lord."

Scott nodded and quirked his lip. "I don't know
why, but she's not the only tough nut around." She
knew he was thinking of his family again. Then he
looked over at her in the dimly lighted booth, the music
swirling around them. "What about you, Nat? Has
anything like that ever happened in your family?"

She gave it some thought. "Several things with some
distant relatives, but nothing in our immediate family.
Sometimes, I wonder how we escaped . . . and how
much longer it will be before something horrible happens—" she looked into the dark eyes and felt herself
melting like the marshmallow on top of her cocoa—"and
will I be strong enough to take it when it does. . . ."

He reached across the table and trapped one of her
hands with his. "You're the greatest, Nat. I can't imagine you ever wimping out. I feel so lucky to know you
. . . to be with you."

She waited it out. She couldn't have said anything anyway for the big lump in her throat.

"I value your opinion, Natalie," Scott went on, gazing earnestly into her eyes. "Do you think I should sign that contract?"

Natalie still didn't trust her voice to work. She grasped the stem of her water glass and hung on. She wanted to say, "What about throwing away the best years of your life? What about missing out on some great times with your friends? What about a special girlfriend in your senior year . . . *me*?" She *wanted* to say all that. But she didn't.

Lord, help me say the right thing. Help me be the friend Scott thinks I am. Help! Finally she forced out the words she knew had to be spoken, even though her voice was kind of thin and quavery. "That has to be your decision, Scott. You know I can't tell you what to do."

"I know. But I'd still like to know what you think."

She sighed deeply. "Did you ask God to close the door if He doesn't want you to go through it?"

"Yeah." He grinned a little sheepishly. "That's one reason I wanted to wait about making the decision. I was waiting for the door to slam."

Natalie smiled feebly. "But it didn't."

The slight movement of his brows and the dropping of his gaze told her what they both knew. The door was wide open.

Then Scott gave a snort and looked across at her. "I'm making too much of this, Nat." His eyes seemed to plead with her to believe that. "It's not like I'd be signing my life away. Our attorney said to counter offer with a six-month contract. That's not too long, is it?"

She shook her head. *Only the rest of our senior year.*

"And signing a contract doesn't mean I'll get any offers. I may only be in a couple of ads or something." He paused. "Or maybe nobody will ask me to model for them at all."

"Apparently the agency thinks you could be a success."

"At least Tony seems to think so." He laughed lightly. After a pause, he added, "Maybe this has happened because he's where I was a few months ago. And maybe my *real* job here is to be as good an influence on him as you've been on me."

Natalie didn't know what to say. "Thanks, Scott. But you made all the decisions—not me."

"You were around, though," he said, now leaning over the table toward her. "You stuck by me when I was a basket case over my mom's alcohol problem . . . and when Zac was facing prison. My whole family owes you, Nat, and none of us will forget you for hanging in there with us."

She shrugged. "It wasn't very hard to do." *Not hard at all. In fact, it's the easiest thing I ever did in my life . . . because I love you, you big lug.*

"I might as well do it."

He'd dropped his voice, so she had to ask him to repeat it. Then he wiped his mouth with the napkin and got to his feet. "You finished?"

I'm finished, all right, in more ways than one. She stood, too, and picked up her jacket.

Walking together toward the elevator, she heard an old Elvis tune. It echoed her sentiments exactly. "I'll have . . . a blue Christmas . . . without you."

The rest of the morning passed in a blur for Natalie, after she finally awoke—late. But no one seemed to notice that she wasn't entering into the conversation when she and Cissy arrived at the suite. Everything was mass confusion. The Carlos had to be notified about Scott's decision. Then when Antonio came for them, he and his mom left for the agency to work out the details of the contract.

Natalie was actually relieved when Elizabeth Stiles mentioned that they'd decided to take an earlier flight to Garden City in the morning. "Seems a winter storm is forecast for the middle of the week. We want to get home before it hits."

Natalie had heard that people with rheumatism could feel an approaching storm "in their bones." Well, she didn't have rheumatism, but she definitely felt the storm warnings in her heart. She wanted to go home—before it *broke.*

Suddenly she missed her dad telling her everything would be all right. And her mom's good, sound advice. She'd always been able to tell her best friend, Ruthie, everything, too. Until lately, that is. Lately, Ruthie had been giving her the cold shoulder. Probably because she felt left out, with Natalie running around with Scott and Cissy so much these days. Anyway, there hadn't been much time for calling home. She'd only called twice—once, to tell her folks she'd arrived safely. And a quick call to Ruthie after the contest.

She'd just have to take her troubles to God. He always knew what to do. . . .

"If you're going shopping, Cissy, you'd better do it

soon," Elizabeth Stiles was saying, returning Natalie's attention to matters at hand, instead of the heart. Then, seeing Cissy's expression, she added, "Honestly, honey, I've never known you to be so indifferent about a chance to spend money."

There were a few chuckles at that, but Cissy didn't say anything until brunch, when, judging from the reaction at the table, her announcement was the last thing any of them were expecting!

"I've decided how I'm going to use the gift certificate from Macy's."

Aunt Helen shot her a curious glance. Scott and Natalie appeared mildly interested. But her mom, coffee cup hovering in midair, was eager to hear more. "Well, tell us . . . what? A new winter coat? A party dress for the holidays? Some more of those jeans you young people live in?"

"None of the above." Cissy watched the eyebrows lift. Even Natalie seemed surprised. "I want to buy Gertrude a new wardrobe."

"Gertrude?!" There was a look of total disbelief all around the table.

"Nat, after you got through telling me what you and Scott were up to last night—the sad shape you found that poor old woman in—you didn't really think I'd spend that money on *myself*, did you?"

Natalie appeared to be flabbergasted. "But . . . you already gave her your coat."

"Oh, that old thing? I'm ashamed to say I've got five more just like it—in different colors. If I bought any more clothes, my dad would have to add an extra room! Come on. Let's go get Gertrude and take her with us. Maybe Antonio will come along, too. This should be fun!"

The next few hours went by with the speed of a supercomputer, Natalie thought, as she helped Gertrude into her new home with a load of packages. After cashing in Cissy's gift certificate and outfitting the old woman in enough warm clothes to hold her till spring, the two women had insisted on spending some of their own money—in Housewares. "She'll need some sheets, towels, blankets, kitchen utensils," Helen had ticked off the items, enough to furnish the two-room apartment, with kitchenette, the caseworker had lined up for her.

"Sure hope the landlord loves pets, 'cause where I go, Patches goes," Gertrude insisted, clinging to the mangy little mutt in her arms.

Just at that moment, Antonio, loaded with groceries, ducked through the door. "I think I can put in a good word for you." He grinned. "I just happen to know the guy personally."

"*You're* the landlord," Natalie whispered, putting two and two together.

"My *dad*." He deposited the sack of groceries on the kitchen table and went back for another.

"So that's how they managed to find an apartment for Gertrude and move her in—all in the same day." Helen Lambert was clearly overwhelmed. "Things like that don't just happen—even in Garden City."

Elizabeth took off her coat. "Let's get organized, Helen. If we don't stand here yakking all day, we could have Gertrude and Patches all set up by suppertime."

And later, when supper was served, no exotic dish Natalie had tried—including veal medallions at the hotel's rooftop restaurant—had ever tasted half as good as spaghetti and meatballs in Gertrude's makeshift kitchen!

With packing yet to do, Helen and Elizabeth begged off "doing the town" on this last night in New York. "But you go ahead."

Antonio was his charming self when he dropped them off at the hotel. "If you ladies don't mind, there's one more place I'd like to show these three. The *piéce de resistance*, so to speak."

"I'll just bet *I* can guess." Elizabeth Stiles was a pushover for Antonio's style, Natalie decided. *Like mother, like daughter,* she thought, seeing Cissy's glowing face and knowing she'd hoped to spend a little more time with him before she left.

She watched the blond heads tilt to take in the city skyline, where the Empire State Building jutted up through the now lowering clouds and towered over other nearby skyscrapers.

Helen Lambert waved them off. "Well, have fun. But don't keep them out too late, Antonio. My *son* needs his beauty sleep!"

The women were still laughing—their laughter trailing behind them like silver bells—all the way through the revolving door of the Marriott.

Thirteen

"As you can see, the top thirty floors of the Empire State Building are illuminated at night." Antonio made like a tour guide again, pointing out the city's major tourist attraction. "On a clear day, it can be seen from fifty miles away."

From the backseat of the Carlos' car, Natalie figured that was about the distance from which *Cissy* could be seen right now. Her smile practically glowed in the dark! But her blue eyes were not on the fabulous structure rising a quarter of a mile into the night sky. They were glued to Antonio, probably memorizing every dent and dimple in his handsome face.

"That building reminds me of an old movie I saw once," Cissy chattered away as Antonio wove through the traffic. "This couple met on a cruise ship, fell in love, and promised that if they still felt the same way in another year, they'd meet on top of the Empire State Building. Well, when the guy got there—exactly one year later—she wasn't there. No note. No nothing."

Cissy sighed. "But here's the best part. He finally tracks her down. And while he's telling her off for leading him on—then not letting him know she changed her mind—he notices that she hasn't moved from the couch. She's just lying there, with an afghan thrown over her legs. When he asks her about it, she admits that on the way to meet him, she'd been struck by a car. So . . . instead of chaining him to a cripple . . . she'd just decided to fade out of his life."

Natalie was hooked. "Well, Cissy? How did it end?"

"*I* know," Antonio spoke up. "The guy agrees not to be tied down, so he leaves. The woman spends the rest of her days on the couch, watching the soaps on TV. Right?"

"You jerk!" Cissy teased. "You don't have a drop of romance in your veins!"

Natalie giggled, then watched Antonio turn to grin at Cissy.

"Hey, buddy, better watch the traffic!" Scott called out as they narrowly missed a Yellow Cab that had swerved in front of them.

"Speaking of traffic," Antonio said, "it's a good thing my father rents space in a parking garage around here. You have heard, haven't you, that New York's been called 'the city of ten million dreams—but only one parking space'?"

They were all chuckling as they left the garage and started down Fifth Avenue toward the entrance of the building. "Brrr, it's getting colder." Antonio hunched his shoulders, then glanced up. "Cloudy too. The city at night is the eighth wonder of the world. But we won't be able to see much of it tonight."

"Who cares?" Cissy shook it off. "At least we can say we've been there."

In the lobby, Natalie picked up a brochure and flipped it open. "Hmmm. The Empire State Building is called the 'cathedral of the skies.' Nice idea."

" 'Some of the elevators operate at speeds ranging up to 1,200 feet a minute,' " Scott read over her shoulder, then did some rapid calculation—"which means that we can be at the top in about a minute! Or . . . we could take the stairs." He squinted at the fine print. "Only 1,860 steps."

At that point, Antonio took charge. "To the elevators, everybody!" he announced firmly. "Everybody but Scott, that is. He'd rather walk."

Laughing, Antonio ducked Scott's fake right hook and led the way to the marble wall, where he pressed a button.

It was a quick trip, just as the brochure had promised. Seconds later, when they got off on the eighty-sixth floor, they found the world at their feet. Along with the snack bar and souvenir counters inside the lobby, there were outdoor promenades on all four sides of the building, with a view of the city stretching as far as the eye could see.

Stepping outside into the brisk breeze, they walked over to the railing. Tonight, New York looked like a bride, Natalie thought, dressed in billowy clouds of white, her eyes sparkling with happy tears—all those millions of twinkling lights—through a veil of fog and mist.

Antonio took another look at the overcast sky. "Too bad. On a clear night, you'd have been able to see for eighty miles in any direction."

This was as good a time as any, so Natalie asked,

"Why is New York called the Big Apple, Antonio?"

"I'm not sure," he admitted with a shrug. "Maybe it's because New York is the second most important apple-producing state in the country."

Cissy seemed thoughtful for a minute. "Since there has to be cross-pollination in order for most apple varieties to bear adequately," she broke in, while Antonio turned to stare, "maybe the apple represents all the ethnic backgrounds in New York that make it so unique."

Antonio was obviously impressed, but this was no surprise to Natalie and Scott. Cissy wasn't just another pretty face. She'd been on the honor roll all four years of high school, been president of the student council, and was an excellent speaker.

Stepping up behind Natalie, Scott put one hand on her shoulder and pointed with the other. "Was that a snowflake I just saw?"

Antonio laughed at his baffled expression. "I wouldn't be surprised. It isn't as if we hadn't been expecting something like this."

"Hey, Nat! How about you and me going all the way to the top?" Scott seemed eager. "Maybe we can find a regular snowstorm!"

Cissy's face brightened, as if she, too, were intrigued by the prospect, then caught Scott's eye and backed off. "I think this is high enough for me, thank you just the same. What about you . . . Tony?"

Antonio hesitated, gave Scott a searching look, then announced decisively, "If *you* stay, young lady, *I* stay."

Natalie glanced around behind her at Scott to see

what was going on with all these long looks. But he was the picture of wide-eyed innocence.

"Let's go." He took her arm and hauled her back inside and over to the elevator.

"Be careful," Antonio called after them. "Anything can happen up there. Sometimes it even snows *up* instead of *down*."

"Then we won't say you didn't tell us ahead of time," Scott called back just as they stepped onto the elevator.

"I think my cousin planned that little getaway," Cissy told Antonio as the elevator door peeled shut. "I think he's been wanting to get Nat alone all week . . . but so much has happened. . . ." She stood, looking into the mist, thinking of the competition, the homeless woman, Kameko's suicide attempt, Gertrude's escape from the shelter. Someone ought to write a book—but nobody would believe it!

"Hey, let's find an overhang somewhere," he said, wiping a splat of frozen rain from his face. "We're going to get wet!"

He steered her to the inside wall of the building, out of the wind. Inside the lobby, only a few last-minute visitors milled about, and most everyone else was filing back in from the observation deck to wait for the elevator.

"You know," Tony began when they were finally alone, "when your cousin offered me his camcorder the night of the . . . accident . . . I figured he was just some naive kid from Podunk. But he's a genuinely nice guy." She waited for him to finish. "Guess I've always prided myself on being a real New Yorker—a man of the world. Now . . . well, I'm not so sure. . . ."

He gazed off into space. "If the accident hadn't happened that night, I probably wouldn't even have noticed Scott. . . ."

"And he wouldn't be on his way to a modeling career," Cissy finished for him.

"Not only that, but I might not have gotten any closer to you than the runway at the Marriott." Apparently Tony suddenly remembered that he was supposed to be this big man of the world, and he moved in until she could feel his warm breath on her cheek. "Looks like fate to me . . . or as you guys would say, 'the will of God.' "

"My eye, too?" She grinned up at him. "But I suppose it was worth it . . . to launch Scott's new career, I mean."

"Let me see that eye." He cupped her face in his hands. She held her breath as he inspected the wound, lightly running his finger over the tender flesh. "Only a very small scar." He dropped his hands to her shoulders. "You're perfectly beautiful."

She tried to toss off a light remark, but her heart was hammering so hard she was sure he could hear it. "You see beautiful girls every day, Tony."

"Yes, but as I've told you before . . . there's something different about you . . . something I'd like to explore."

"I'm leaving in the morning," she reminded him.

"You'll be back"—was he daring her?—"if only to see Scott. Besides, transportation goes both ways."

"You wouldn't be fishing for an invitation to Garden City, would you?"

He lifted one dark brow. "Oh, I expect to get an invitation from your cousin . . . but I wouldn't accept unless I knew someone else wanted me there, too."

"Oh . . . I do!" Her breathless whisper was almost like a vow.

A shadow crossed his eyes, and his fingers tightened on her shoulders just as a gust of freezing air blew in from around the corner. "Let's go inside." For no apparent reason, his voice took on a tone as cold and impersonal as the weather.

She shivered. What on earth had she said to bring about *that* sudden change of atmosphere?

Natalie saw only one other couple—over by the high-powered binoculars—when she and Scott stepped out onto the 102nd floor observatory deck. Surprisingly, except for an occasional gust, the wind had died down.

Anything can happen! Antonio had said.

Would she see it snowing up instead of down?

But she knew Scott hadn't brought her here to see some natural phenomenon. This was good-bye. He would tell her—again—what a great friend she'd been. Icy moisture struck her face and she shivered, feeling as cold inside as a snowman.

"So what do you think of New York?" Scott asked, coming up to stand beside her at the protective outside wall.

Natalie squinted at the view, partially blocked by the clouds that were now spitting flurries of snow. Up here, the air was thin, a little like the mountains of

North Carolina where her grandparents lived. At some of the scenic overviews there, you could see forever, too. But those views were of gently sloping hills and valleys, curving mountain roads, winding streams—all soft and rounded—created by God. Here everything was hard and angular—and manmade. "It's a great place to visit. . . ."

" . . . but you wouldn't want to live here," he finished the familiar quotation.

"No . . . but *you* would." A wisp of passing cloud left its damp imprint—like a good-bye kiss—on her face.

"Not if I had to live in a rundown apartment or a slum . . ." he paused, "or an alley. But with the opportunities I have, Natalie, I admit it looks promising. There's something exciting about trying to make it in a big city. It's a real challenge, even though it may not be the safest thing to do."

She darted him a quick glance. "Are you worried about the crime rate here?"

Bracing his arms on the ledge, he leaned over and looked down at his shoes. "Not really. It would be . . . safer . . . to take the route my family—at least my *dad*—has always wanted me to go."

"Become a doctor?"

He nodded and straightened, still holding on to the ledge. "Yeah. It's a family tradition. And it makes sense. Zac and I could go through med school together, since he's had to postpone his schooling for a couple of years while he's doing community service work. I could get the first few years of college out of the way right there in southern Illinois, and be"—he shoved his hands into his jacket pockets and looked over at her—"close to *you*."

Suddenly the air was even thinner, making it difficult to get a deep breath. "You . . . you thought about that?"

He nodded. "That's been the hardest part, Natalie. Feeling like I might be losing you. You're the best thing that ever happened to me."

She couldn't believe her ears. He liked her, he really *liked* her!

"Now, I'm going to have to be away a lot. It's exciting," he confessed. "Scary too. Things have already changed so much. I keep wondering if it's all a dream."

"It's no dream, Scott . . . it's real. And you deserve every bit of it."

He scuffed his shoe against the concrete floor, hands still in his pockets. "Oh, I doubt that, but somehow it seems wrong to turn down the opportunity. I just didn't expect to have to make such important decisions so soon." He looked up then. "I wanted to have fun, to be sort of carefree for a while . . . you know? Do things together. We've been though some pretty heavy stuff."

He freed his hands and pulled her around to face him. "I don't ever want to lose you, Natalie."

She didn't care anymore if he could read her feelings on her face. She felt as light as the snowflakes now, softly falling all around.

"You're turning white," he said with a little laugh.

She laughed back. "So are you."

He led her next to the shelter of the inner wall, but he didn't take his hand away. "You remember that movie Cissy was talking about on the way over here?"

Movie? What movie? This was the real thing. Scott's chocolate brown eyes gazing deep into hers. The thick, swirling flakes shutting out the rest of the world.

"The promise that couple made," he prompted. Then he said it again. "Nat, I'm serious. I don't ever want to lose you."

Her heart was thudding so hard she couldn't speak.

"We'll have four years of college after high school, right?"

"Y-yes," she choked out.

"No matter what happens, I'll want to know what's going on with you. You think we could . . . promise to meet here four years from now?" He ducked his head and added quickly, "Unless you think it's a dumb idea."

She finally found her voice. "Dumb? I think it's an awesome idea, Scott." Where had *that* word come from? She usually refused to use some of the hip words the other kids tossed around. "And if something happens that one of us can't make it, we could send a note, or call and leave a message."

His face came alive. "Let's set a date."

"Graduations are over by the first week in June. What about the second week? Say . . . June 8?"

Scott's smile lit up the night. "It's a date. June 8 . . . four years from now." He pulled her close. "You know what Gertrude said—I don't intend to let you get away . . . not if I can help it. Nat . . . I love you."

"Oh, Scott," she breathed, hardly aware of the snow falling all around them—fluttering like little doves' wings in the air.

So this is love, Natalie thought. While the snow was softly falling—so was she . . . so was he. She could see it in his eyes, in his face, in his smile. This was first love, true love, pure love. She'd cherish this moment in her heart . . . forever—like the photographs she'd take home for her album to remember this trip.

Down below, even though it was late, the city throbbed with life. Ten million hearts were beating—but not as fast as hers. Ten million people were dreaming dreams—but hers were coming true.

Scott tugged her close and held her. They stood, listening to the stillness, drawing warmth from each other. Then he tipped her chin toward his and lowered his head.

Just before his lips met hers in a promise of commitment, she whispered, "I love you, Scott . . . and I always will."

She felt like a snowflake—melting!

Isn't the senior year of high school supposed to be "the best year of your life"? So why has it been such a bummer for Ruthie Ryan? Her relationship with Sean Jacson is falling apart, and she can't even talk to her best friend, Natalie, about it. Natalie's too busy falling in love, while Sean is treating Ruthie badly, even abusively. To make matters worse, the last person on earth she'd ever want to know about her troubles, *knows*! What's going on anyway? Find out in *A Fighting Chance,* WHITE DOVE ROMANCE #5.